Blood Stone

BY

MELACHI TAYLOR

Editors: *Antrina Richardson, BookedRight Editing Services*

Interior Designer: *Lissha Sadler*

Cover Designer: *K and T Graphics and AMB Branding*

ISBN-10:1-945999-00-4

ISBN-13:978-1-945999-00-0

Our books may be purchased in bulk for promotional, educational or business use. Please contact your local bookseller or
Rhys World Media Group LLC
1273 Metropolitan Avenue, Suite 160121
Atlanta, GA 30316
rhysworldpublishing.com

ACKNOWLEDGEMENTS

To my loved ones who are with God in Heaven, my Granny Fran, my auntie Pamela "Mickey" Taylor, my sister Tiffany Taylor, my first love Mary Davis, and my favorite girl to talk to Heather "Mz. Bookie Baby" Davis. All of you were taken too soon from us, but I swear y'all left the most beautiful memories and they'll transcend time. Y'all will always be missed. I love y'all and this one right here is for y'all. To my kids Gregory, Jordan, Lexi, Tasia, Noah, and Mikaylee Skittles, I swear to never miss another birthday or graduation ceremony. I know what has to be done and I'm doing it. Y'all are the reason I breathe and I love y'all with every fiber of who I am.

To my critics thuggin' it out in the system: Myran "Sniper" Snyder, Jeffery "Bo Dean" Lewis, Clay Gilmer, Marcus " Liver Lips" Davis, Tyrone "Cee-Lo" Collins, Cornelius "Money" Thomas, and Green "who knows the bullshit truth better" Cornbread, y'all niggaz kept it real with me from day one about my books and couldn't wait to get y'all hands on the next one. And for that reason it kept me writing. Without y'all I'm nothing. I'll never forget y'all. You niggaz won't ever have to buy one of these joints off the shelf if I'm in the store with you, lol! To my brothers, Jermaine "Catfish" Johnson, Deon Johnson, Michael Irvin, Reggie "Moldy Frog" Brown, and Bruce "Pimpin Pippy" Modicue, without y'all making sure my books stayed cool when y'all could, I would not have been able to send out my manuscript. Know what I'm saying Big Top? I love y'all.

A special shout out to Wilma Taylor. To tell you that I love you is not enough. You've been there for me since the days of me having to sleep in my car and never once judged me for anything except being a playa, lol. Thank you so much for your love and support. Nay can't spend my first check…. To Karla Elliott, thank you for getting in touch with me. Without your first email, I never would've made this connection with Rhys World and Lissha. So, thank you publication mate. And thank you Rhys World for taking a chance and making me family. I won't let you down. My mind gonna stay sick as shit to give this writing game a lil something different to vibe out to. The best of me ain't even came out yet. My joints get better from here on out. Ain't no watered-down shit gone be the legacy I leave behind.

I want to thank the fan I don't have in advance. Y'all about to love this shit. Promise. Check out Reggie A. Brown on YouTube because he shootin' my first short movie as soon as I touch. Real soon. This is our time. Melachi has found a home at Rhys World and it's finna be a ma'fuckin take over.

LETS GET IT!
Melachi- BLOODLINE- LIFE 4 A LIFE

Blood Stone

By

Melachi Taylor

PROLOGUE

Shaka was ruthless, but Mika didn't know the extent of just how ruthless until this nigga blew her grandmother's head off with a double barrel shotgun. Blood, brains, and bone painted and peppered the family pictures grapefruit pink and red on the wall behind her. Mika fought against the duct tape restraints binding her to the chair. She was completely helpless. One of Shaka's goons stood behind her forcing her to look at his boss' gruesome display of revenge. Mika made threats, but Shaka's damage had been done and there was no taking it back.

A single tear trailed down her swollen and bruised cheek when her grandmother's headless body hit the floor with a dry thud and began to jerk violently. This wasn't the first time she had been a witness to death. Lord knows she put in much work with this nigga back in the day, but this was different on a whole other level. This was her grandmother, an innocent person. She was a woman who devoted her entire life to the neighborhood church and the upbringing of the whole hood.

There wasn't a child or adult who didn't know and love Ms. Della. And if the corrupted soul in this nigga could be so cold and callous as to turn her innocent, well-loved grandmother's head into potted meat, she could only imagine what he had in store for her. But being the boss bitch that she was she refused to beg a bitch nigga like Shaka for her life.

Mika squared her shoulders back and was ready to take her dome call like a real bitch.

"Kill me, bitch ass nigga!" she spat with venom, hoping at that very moment that he would make good on her demand so that he would end the pain her heart was enduring.

Shaka turned to Mika and smirked. He kneeled in front of her, propped on his toes, and passed the sawed off to one of the henchmen to the right of him.

"Now why would I do that," he asked cynically. "That would defeat the purpose of you feelin' my wrath upon your life." He stood to his full height of 6'2.

"Let's go," he commanded his two henchmen. They casually walked out the front just as calmly and smoothly as they walked in.

Mika turned her head away from the deadly scene of her grandmother lying on the floor in a pool of blood in front of her. She let her head dip low for a moment of silence, then lifted it with a renewed strength and made a promise aloud. She would get her revenge on Shaka, and she would serve it to him cold.

CHAPTER 1

In the beginning, Shaka and Mika were inseparable. She mimicked him so much, that she could finish his sentences. They were always thinking alike, even when it came to the capers they pulled. Shaka would find the mark then send Mika in to do her thang. There wasn't a soul between here and Heaven who could resist her. That applied to bitches too. The price for licking pussy for a dyke bitch clocking paper was costly. Mika didn't give a fuck. There were no exceptions. Money talked and bullshit ran a thousand miles.

Shaka had the baddest, blackest bitch in Flood County, IL. a.k.a. the Flux. That was until he caught them football numbers and she shook Shaka's ass for the next best thing.

"When you used to living a certain lifestyle, you don't wanna be known as the bitch that fell off, ya feel me?" Mika stated to her homegirl, Tiara, as they rode around the Flux in her brand new pearl gray Audi A8 L, smoking a blunt of White Willow.

"I feel you, bitch," the seventeen-year-old Tiara replied with her extra girly voice that matched her beautiful mulatto features. "But pass that blunt while you run your spill. A bitch tryin' ta smoke."

Mika passed the blunt. "Here bitch."

"So how long that nigga Shaka get anyways?" she asked nonchalantly.

"Hellas is all I know." But in all actuality, Shaka was still in his trial process. The shiesty bitch just left him for dead.

Tiara hit the blunt and talked over her intake. "I know that nigga hella mad you left him in there for dead, huh?" she asked as though she were reading Mika's mind.

Mika laughed. "Hell yeah. Makin' def threats and some mo' shit 'bout how he gone kill me for playin' him." More laughter.

"Shit, that nigga ain't ever gone see the light of day again. He just need to concentrate on not droppin' that soap," she laughed.

Tiara passed the blunt back. "How he figured out you played him anyways? I know he didn't expect a bitch to hold a nickel between her knees and do life with his dumb ass."

"Hell naw, bitch, it ain't that. That nigga mad cuz I took all his dough and started fuckin' wit his main man Bogus. He feels like that's a slap in his face." Tiara shook her head. Mika looked over and rolled her eyes.

"Ain't no need in you shakin' yo head, bitch. I got that nigga a lawyer and fattened up his books before I left. If that nigga wanted to keep this pussy, then he woulda kept his ass out here where it's at," she said, knowing the only reason he was even in jail was because he stuck his neck out there for her.

"Fuck, I learned how to be grimy from his ass. You know how many times I done been to the clinic, bitch?" Mika didn't give her time to answer and rolled her eyes.

"Too many. Shit, I'm still watchin' for cluster blisters every day so I don't give this nigga Bogus herpes." Tiara fell out laughing.

"Bitch you ill. That shit sound crazy."

"Bitch, I'm fa'real." They laughed together and finished smoking.

Mika dropped Tiara off at her mom's crib on 52nd and Rosebud, but before getting out the car she asked Mika, "Can I borrow those vanilla Jimmy Choos with the gold laces to go with this fly ass Prada skirt and jacket I got for my school dance next Friday?"

"I don't give a fuck girl, matter of fact, you can come raid my closet tomorrow when I come pick yo lil ass up from school. It's time for Bogus to pay his pussy bill anyways, and what better way than with a fall wardrobe, feel me?"

Tiara giggled and shook her head. "That's why I fucks with you. You's a real bitch. Pun intended."

Mika smiled. "It's all good."

Yeah, Tiara was perfect for Mika because unlike most bitches, she wasn't in competition with her. She did her own thing her own way and Mika appreciated that. Tiara was the little sister she never had and she would do anything for her, especially if it meant keeping her from becoming a grimy bitch like herself.

Mika tried calling Bogus' cell phone, not to check in, because she wasn't the one for that bullshit, but to see where he was so she wouldn't run into his jealous ass while she was out doing her. She was sent straight to voicemail. She giggled. "He must be trying to get his lil dick wet somewhere." Mika could care less what he did long as he didn't sponsor some other bitch with his chips. She hit the garage door open application on her cell phone as she came up the block to her home on Tiffany. Bogus didn't know anything about this house and never would if left up to her.

Mika felt at ease when she made it to her two-story home in Glory, just outside the Flux. She was truly grateful that she'd made the purchase when Shaka took his fall from grace. She pulled into her spacious two-car garage and let the white door slide down behind her taillights. She then killed the engine.

Inside the house, Mika kicked off her loafers by the back door and threw her Coach purse on the glass kitchen table as she scurried to get her bare feet off the cool marble floor and onto the carpeted living room floor. She walked around the huge beige leather sectional and flopped down, simultaneously grabbing the remote from the ivory and brass coffee table in front of her. Tucking her feet underneath her butt to warm them, she turned on her sixty-four-inch flat screen mounted on the wall above the fireplace and began to flip through the channels.

She was just about to get into the Bad Girls Club marathon when her cell rang. She reluctantly got up from her warm spot on the couch, slid on her Garfield with the big head slippers, and went to retrieve her phone from her purse on the kitchen table. She looked at the caller I.D. and frowned when she saw that it was Nikki.

Nikki was a Latina chic who Mika had purposely met at the Make a Dolla strip club while checking for this Puerto Rican papi named Rubio, who she knew was Nikki's man. But not just anybody could get to Rubio. He was plugged with the Latin King mob and had security on him tighter than Purple Rain's ass cheeks. So, Mika got at Nikki to make shit happen. Little did Mika know at the time that the Kings had their own hit out on Rubio, and her plan to rob him would never play out. By then she had already started fucking around with Nikki and had the bitch sprung. Even after Rubio was rubbed out the picture, she continued to be pleasured by the Latina stripper. Though Mika would never admit it, she liked Nikki right back because she had that "I'll cut a bitch" attitude about herself. A down-ass hood bitch that could eat pussy better than any nigga she ever came across. All in all, in Mika's close-knit world, Nikki was a keeper.

"Hey mami," Nikki said seductively as soon as Mika picked up.

"Hey," Mika responded dryly.

"Can we meet at the BMF so I can run some shit by you?"

Mika knew that by Nikki not wanting to talk on the phone whatever needed to be discussed had to be about business, so she was game to meet being that she was only sitting on seventy g's at the moment and needed to get her bank back right. She wanted to stay close to, if not more than, a hundred grand at all times because she knew that as long as she did she could bounce or bounce back if she needed to.

"I'll be there. Gimme an hour to freshen up."

"Cool..."

CHAPTER 2

Daku was born in the slums of Tanzania, Southeast Africa, on March 17, 1990. A young woman scavenging for goods discovered him in a trash heap near the local watering hole. Her heart went out to the baby boy she saw surrounded by black rats eating at his purple umbilical cord and copper colored feet. She literally had to kick them away from their fresh meal. "Scat!" she demanded in her native tongue as she picked the baby up from the trash, wrapped him in her red, and white polka dot head garment.

The girl, whose name was Shasta, really couldn't afford to take the baby home. She was barely able to feed her two younger brothers and aged grandmother. Her mother had long ago abandoned them and her father, she assumed, had been killed in the war. Making a living for her family was hard enough without another mouth to feed, especially a baby. But she couldn't just leave the baby to die at the teeth of savage rats.

She quickly got the baby home and bathed him with what clean water she had left in the bucket, then bandaged his feet and tied off his umbilical cord. She had no idea how she would feed him and she knew that he must be hungry because he hadn't stopped crying since she'd found him.

Shasta's grandmother Autu shuffled miserably to what would be considered the kitchen area of the tiny mud hut where tattered garments hung low from clotheslines to dry. She brushed the damp materials aside and made her way to Shasta and the baby. Shasta was seated on a damaged wooden apple crate, as she turned to look over her shoulder when she heard her grandmother approach.

"Grandmother, you should be in bed. You are not well," she said properly to her grandmother. An American female student with white skin, blue eyes and a Christian faith taught her how to speak properly whenever she found time to sneak away, which was nearly three to four times a week.

"Shasta, when you get to be my age den you can tell me what to do." Autu came to stand beside Shasta. She plucked the baby from her arms. "He's hungry, Shasta. Where he mutter?"

"I'm sorry to say Grandmother, but I found him in the trash while fetching water and scavenging for food."

Autu was making her way back through the hut, almost dancing through the tattered garments hanging from the clotheslines. She began singing to the baby. "Shasta, we will call him Daku, and you can stop calling me Grandmother. I am Autu."

"Yes, Grandmother." Autu humphed. "But Daku?" Shasta asked brightly. "What does the name mean, Grandmother?" she asked, as if the name held some type of glorified weight.

"Nothin' chile. He just looks like he should be named Daku."

In Tanzania life was harsh, but the few dogs that had homes found themselves well off because they ate any and every scrap they could find to fatten up. That was why Bananas, the mixed with everything breed that Kenji and Rahmi, Shasta's kid brothers, brought home had her weight up and had given birth to six healthy puppies who were now seven weeks old.

Autu heard Kenji and Rahmi outside the hut playing with the dogs. "Kenji," she called out to the oldest of the eight-year old twins. "Come yea and bring dat Bananas with you, ya 'ear?"

"Yes, Granny Tutu," he responded cheerfully.

Rahmi stayed outside playing with the puppies running all around as Kenji did what Autu had asked of him. When he made his way in, he saw that Autu had a baby bundled in her arms. He looked from Autu to Shasta then back at Autu before he called out, "Rahmi, Shassy done had a baby!"

Rahmi instantly ran into the hut followed by the litter of pups and said "Shassy had a baby and Granny Tutu didn't beat she?"

"You two boys are too grown for you own age," Autu said to them with a comical grin.

"Yes, too grown," Shasta agreed, taking both her brothers by the arms leading them outside the hut, puppies in tow. "Now stay out here and play, understand?"

"But we hungry, Shassy," they pleaded, stomachs growling.

"Well eat one of those cute puppies," she teased.

They both looked at each other incredulously. "Can we fa'real?"

"NO! Now go play."

"Yes, Shassy."

As she walked back inside she could hear Kenji ask Rahmi, "Do you think the old witch will cook up a pup for us if we ask?"

"I'm tellin' when we get back, Kenji. You can't eat my puppies."

Kenji pushed his twin. "Cry baby."

Shasta laughed at her brothers, but she had been seriously considering barbecuing the two healthiest puppies for days now.

"Shasta," Autu called out, killing her thoughts of crispy puppy skin. "Turn dat dare dog over so dat dis baby can suckle milk." Shasta's brow furrowed with a crazy look on her face. "Don't look at me like dat chile. Unless you have milk in dem juvenile teats of your own, I suggest you do as I say so's we can get this baby fed."

Shasta couldn't believe what Autu had asked of her, but what choice did she have? At this point, milk was milk, even if was a dog's milk. She gently flipped Bananas on her side and soothed her with chest and leg rubs while Autu helped Daku latch on to one of her healthy nipples to suckle. Bananas didn't seem to mind and Daku's cries were immediately hushed. Both women had satisfied looks on their faces.

"For awhile you will make sure dis dog eats a fair share of our best pickings so dat Daku is strong. He is a survivor like us and will get his due," Autu said sincerely as she rose to her feet, leaving Daku bundled up on the floor in a white cloth sucking Banana's titty. He started to drift off.

"I'm going to rest now. You should be okay from 'ere. Send you brothers to gather firewood so's you can burn a couple of those pups too with dem oats you found."

For Daku, growing up this way was very humbling and normal because he'd never known any other life outside of the one he was living to compare it to. But what normality he did know was stripped away from him at the tender age of nine when a legion of rebels stormed their peaceful village. Kenji, now seventeen, burst into the hut screaming, "'Ide yourself and Daku quickly," his deep African accented voice commanded Shasta.

"Where's Rahmi, Kenji?" she asked in a panic, then began to cry.

Kenji held his big sister by the shoulders and looked her in the eyes. "I dunno. I pray he's okay, but I need you to pool it togethah and 'ide." He tried to turn her in the opposite direction, but she was unmoving. He kissed her forehead. "It'll

14

be okay, Shassy, promise." But his eyes told a different story. Shasta couldn't shake the reality of it all. She took Daku by the hand and led him into the kitchen area where she had been hand-washing clothes in a large metal bucket with stones.

"Hide under this pile of clothes little one and no matter what you hear, do not move, okay?" Daku's bulging brown eyes welled up and spilled over. He was speechless and shaking his head no, so Shasta shook him and began to cry uncontrollably herself.

"Please, Daku, please! You have to hide. This is important. I love you. Promise me you won't move." He stood stock-still. Shasta shook him again with urgency.

"Promise me!" Daku nodded his head yes. Shasta pulled him close and hugged him with all her might. "Now get under these clothes and don't move, okay." He nodded and she quickly covered him up with all the clothes then ran back to Kenji.

Gunshots rang out in multiples. The panic in the screaming voices mingled with the cacophony of madness. Shasta knew that chaos was headed their way. She would either be a slave by nightfall or dead within the next few moments. Kenji had wanted his sister to hide, but she would not so he hugged her instead. He had already embraced his fate an hour before when he witnessed the father of a household being mercilessly hacked to death by men with machetes in the middle of a crowded street, while the rebels cheered from the sidelines. At that moment, he decided to fight the rebels with whatever weapon he could find, hoping that he would be shot in order to get it over with quickly.

Shasta released Kenji when three rebels, dressed in black camo with red bandannas tied around their heads and left biceps, burst through the opening of the hut waving their AK-47s. In their native tongue, they demanded that they lay down.

Kenji was a bit too swift for the first rebel through the opening, so when he came up with the knife he'd been holding at his side, he stabbed the rebel in the throat and then came down into the second rebel's chest. The only choice the third one had was to open fire. He riddled Kenji with bullets and dropped him. More rebels poured in. Shasta ran over to her brother's lifeless body and tried to pick him up and talk him back to life. Pink and purple foam bubbled from his mouth and ran down the side of his sinking face. The third rebel kicked her away as hard as he could. The new rebels snatched her up from the floor and began to toss her to each other with force, making sexual noises and licking out their tongues like snakes.

"Hold her!" the third rebel ordered. A couple of them did as he instructed. He approached her. Shasta snatched away and slapped him hard across the face. The sting was a wakeup call to all the senses in his skin. He immediately returned her slap with the back of his hand, knocking her to the floor. "Pick her up!"

Her legs were wobbly. The rebel ripped her shirt completely off in one motion. He then pulled out his massive black dick.

They all raped Shasta's virgin pussy and ass repeatedly. When they were done, they killed her with five shots to the head. Daku watched all of this from beneath the pile of clothing and did not move for fear he would be killed, and if he were killed, who would avenge his family?

CHAPTER 3

BMF Burgers stood for Big Ma'fuckin' Burgers. Although technically the acronym stood for Big Mama Franks, the hood always had a way of twisting things. The place puts you in the mind of Varsity down in Atlanta on Peachtree, but with a smaller parking lot. The place was packed, even though it was an early Thursday evening and school had not long let out. The youngsters liked to hang out and chop it up about what went on during school and how they planned to spend their weekend. A few of the older baller niggaz clocked dough selling weed or E pills. Their older perverted asses only came around to run game on the younger up and coming prospects they knew they could sell an empty dream to.

Nikki was seated in a booth at the back of the restaurant and waved Mika over when she saw her come through the glass double doors. Even though Mika had played the dress-down role and put on a Prada denim pants outfit and Manolo Timbs, she was still the Flux's favorite eye candy, and all eyes were on her before the doors could even close behind her. But not all eyes had love in them, though not one bitch dared to cross that line knowing Mika stayed strapped. The .32 derringer belt buckle wasn't just for show. She sauntered over to where Nikki was and gave her a warm hug.

"Hey gurl," Mika greeted her homie, lover, and friend.

"Hey back to you," Nikki responded with smiling eyes.

Mika slid into the booth, seating herself across from her. "So what you on draggin' me out the crib and away from my relax time?" Mika asked with a weary smile.

Nikki winked at her and returned the smile, singing, "You know meee..."

Which meant that Nikki had one helluva lick for the two of them and that Mika would be just as excited as she was when she learned what it was. Mika hated the anticipation, but couldn't let on that she was perturbed with Nikki holding out because boss bitches didn't do the emotions on the sleeve thing. So in response she asked, "Have you ordered yet?" This was done to relinquish the power that Nikki presumed to have over her by intentionally withholding information. Mika knew that this calculated maneuver would do two things.

First, it showed that she wasn't pressed. You know, never sweat the small shit. And second, make Nikki wanna spill her guts. In which she did, but only after they had eaten and Mika was drying the blunt with her lighter as they sat on a park bench under a pavilion in New Lawn Park where Nikki trailed Mika to in her '06 Nissan Maxima.

"Don't you wanna know what's cookin' in Nikki's kitchen?"

I would've liked to know that as soon as we met, Mika thought, putting the blunt between her lips and firing up while her free hand cupped around the lighter's flame to shield it from the wind. "Yeah, go ahead and run yo spill. I'm listening," she said apathetically while she hope she'd taught Nikki a little something about getting down to business from jump street.

"So peep game," she began excitedly. "I'm at work the other night shakin' my money maker at The Tip Drill. You know, T -Bill n 'em spot down on Greg and Seventh." Mika nodded then exhaled the chronic smoke. She gestured with her hand for Nikki to continue.

"Anyways, the night was slow as fuck so me and some cool ass white bitches, cuz you know all T -Bill n 'em fuck wit is them white hoes, anyways, we sittin' round popping E, drinking, and talkin' mad shit when this hodgepodge of Zimunda niggaz came in wearin' lions and tigers and shit like them ma'fuckas did in *Coming to America*."

"So," Mika said stoically, trying to pass the blunt.

"Nah," Nikki refused, pushing the blunt away. Mika hunched her shoulders and kept on smoking.

"Would you listen?"

"I am bitch, but you ain't sayin' shit."

Nikki rolled her eyes and blew a fuck you breath out. "Anyway, like I was sayin, rude ass. These Zimunda niggaz come in all garbed up and shit, and when I tell you these ma'fuckas looked intimidating, these ma'fuckas looked like high class killas. All scowled up and shit, plus the crocodile cuts in they faces didn't make it no better."

"They were from Africa tho, bitch?" Mika teased sarcastically, smiling.

"Yea, Mommia, would you listen?" Mika hunched her shoulders again. Nikki continued. "Like I was sayin', the manager, Ball, you know the fat nigga down there always pushin' up on a bitch wit his pinky dick ass, was flaggin', tellin' a couple of us girls to go over after these dudes sat in VIP. So, me and this big booty white chic, Carmen, stroll over all sexy and shit, makin' sho these niggaz see we popping that shit, and I'm throwin' this ass so right that a dick gone puke just thinkin' bout touchin' the lips of this fire pussy, ya heard?" Mika high fived Nikki and they laughed.

Now Nikki wanted the blunt. She hit it a few times and then continued her spill. "So we make it over to these niggaz tables and shit. They poppin' bottles of Dom P and Chrissy like it ain't shit. So while me and Carmen puttin' on our show, I'm thinkin', these niggaz gots to be caked the fuck up."

"Ya think?"

"And sho as shit stank, come to find out these niggaz own some diamond mines in Africa."

Mika snatched her blunt back. "How in the fuck do you know they wasn't sellin' you no bullshit?"

21

"Because," Nikki said, going into her True Religion pocket pulling out a small marble sized diamond. She showed it to Mika. "I had it appraised this morning and they told me its worth at least two hundred twenty-five thousand."

Mika jumped off the bench and took the diamond from Nikki's hand. "You bullshitin' me right now."

"No, Mommia, it's real and the little one that gave it to me says he did it to show me that he genuinely wanted to get to know me while they were in town on business. Plus, he paid me well before they left."

"How much?" Mika asked feverishly.

"Ten stacks."

"Ten stacks bitch, and you ain't fuck and suck this nigga?" Mika was overwhelmed.

"Bitch this a real lick fa'real fa'real. When you spose to hook up with him? We can ransom that nigga." And that's when Nikki grew solemn.

"See, Mommia, that's the catch. You fixin' to trip out."

"About what?" Mika asked inquisitively, holding the diamond up to admire it between her thumb and index.

"You see, dem niggaz didn't come to town on no pleasure ride, they came lookin' for somebody."

"Who?"

"Well, you remember how when we used to pillow talk and you told me about that lame you ran off on?"

"Yeah, Shaka. Wha—" Mika paused. "Bullshit."

"Apparently a relative of his had a stake in the diamond mines and was killed and Shaka is the last family member of his bloodline. So that nigga Shaka that you was fuckin' with is about to be filthy ass rich soon as they find him."

Mika's mind was working a thousand miles an hour plus overtime. She began to pace and smoke. This shit was crazy.

How that lame ass nigga finna be worth millions, maybe even billions, and I ain't gone get my share, she thought.

Aw hell naw. She turned to Nikki and held her by the shoulders, looking deep into her eyes.

"You sure you didn't tell them where Shaka at?"

"Yea. I was waiting for you to tell me the next move because that was your nigga, not mine. So, I told the nigga I could find out all he wanted to know and that it would be wise to wait on me and not put that kinda info in the streets, just in case this Shaka character wasn't a real likable person out here in these streets, feel me?"

Mika felt like she had just been baptized and promised a fa'sho seat up in Heaven when Nikki said that. She kissed Nikki's forehead and lips hard enough to burst them, then smiled profoundly.

"That was so fuckin' smart on your part. Goddamn, that was smart. I'm so fuckin' in love with you right now." She took Nikki by the hand and led her towards their cars.

"Come on, I got some thinking to do and I can do that much better on my back," she giggled.

Bogus was blowing Mika's phone up, but ever since Nikki had put her up on game, she was on some fuck a nigga shit.

I might never get back at you playa, she thought, killing her cell phone for the night.

Nikki had her on her back eating her pussy and ass like melting ice cream while she grabbed at her mauve colored silk sheets and gyrated her hips slowly on Nikki's face.

"Oh, my God. You're suckin' my shit so good, Nikki. Oh fuck, that's my spot right there," Mika yelled in ecstasy, grabbing Nikki's hair to grind harder in her face.

"More...more... oh God, you a boss bitch, Nikki," she shrilled. They carried on back and forth this way until they were both spent, sweating and breathing heavily; enjoying the sentiments of coming down as they lay beside one another.

Mika was lying buck ass on top of the sheets with her legs wide so that her pussy could get some air. She wove her fingers over her pelvic area and shuddered as her body continued to react from cumming so much.

Staring at the ceiling she began, "You know what, we don't have much time before them niggaz find out where Shaka at." She rolled onto her side and propped herself up on an elbow to look at Nikki as she spoke. "The way I see it, we need more time. At least two weeks."

Nikki was lying on her back toying with her swollen brown nipples as if she'd just discovered them. "Two weeks?" She pushed her titties together.

"Yeah, at least. So, what you gotta do is stall the lil one out for us."

"And how I'm gonna do that? We don't even know how long they gonna be in the states."

"Well, you gonna have to convince the lil one to use his juice card with his fellow men. You know, make him convince his people that they should kick back and enjoy America while business is being taken care of. Tell him you will find out all he needs to know and put that pussy and throat muscle on his ass so righteously that he ain't gonna wanna leave without you, feel me?" Nikki was still toying with her herself. Mika gave her a shove. "You feel me?"

Nikki smiled confidently. "I got this."

CHAPTER 4

Daku found himself in a concentration camp at the age of twelve. The year was 2002. A time when freedom was upheld all over the world except for the remote bush where Daku was confined inside a gated compound close to one of Africa's beaches. Two twelve foot fences ran parallel to each other for miles it seemed, to make a square with razor wire doing the loopty loop on both top and bottom. There was no escape. Two guards drove the perimeter in army jeeps while others perambulated with their AK-47s hanging from their shoulder by way of a strap. Some of the guards were as young as thirteen years old.

Housing for the slaves and refugees were hut-like bunkers lined along a piece of land facing away from the mountains and wooded area in the back of them. Inside the bunkers were bunks made of dried mud and straw with about eight inches between them and raised three feet above ground level. Hand crafted hammocks hung about also. There was an indescribable stench that no amount of bleach could kill because what served as the bathroom for these people were holes in the ground. When a hole was filled with the shit of the captives, they'd cover it up with flowers, spices, and mud, and then dig another. Living conditions were even harsher for those who were unable to work in the diamond mines, but for the ones who could, the

26

only difference was the convenience of their shit hole being outside behind the bunker. But everyone bathed with the water hose.

Daku, and what seemed like a hundred others, had just jumped out the back of one of the military work trucks that took them to and from the diamond mines. They were shoved hard, each one of them, by a guard using the butt of his AK as they exited the truck to form a line along the fence. Another guard stood at the entrance of the gate, counting them as they passed through. Once everyone was counted and the gate was secure, the guard raised his hand and the trucks pulled off, leaving a trail of black smoke behind.

Daku's boots were too big for him and were covered in mud while his torn clothes and dark skin were covered in black soot. All he wanted to do was to be sprayed down with the hose and put something clean on before the last meal was brought around. Luckily for him he got his wish then went inside the bunker where he did his pushups and pull-ups. Though he was only twelve, he had a body that put the older men to shame. He stood 5' 5" and was a solid one sixty-five. Daku was cut up like a smaller version of Alex Wheeler. Call it genetics, but he looked like he could seriously fuck something up.

After he finished his daily workout ritual, Daku walked out of his bunker with his tin food pan to stand in line with the others. As always, the workers ate first. It was believed that they needed their strength to work the mines, and after them, the women and children would fight for what was left. Daku ate last every day. He would go without if it meant that one child or woman wouldn't have to go without food. He stood with about seven women and children at the back of the line and the server was already scraping the bottom of the black pot for the last of the slop. Daku was disappointed, but he'd managed to bring a potato back with him from the mines. It wasn't much, but he would make it 'til the next day. The food server tilted the heavy black pot to the side and scraped the last of its contents to the bottom. He had spooned it up and was readying to put into a woman's tin for her and her child when a boy about seventeen or eighteen reached his tin over hers to receive the last of the food after he'd already had his portion. The boy laughed and ran off to demolish what little was left and nobody said a word. The young female child began to cry as her mother consoled her by rubbing her back as they walked away with the last of the broken line. This infuriated Daku, who was usually withdrawn and rarely spoke. Though he wasn't friendly, he was respectful and believed every individual should get what they had coming to them.

Daku took the potato from his pocket and gave it to the woman and her child. "Here," was all he said, placing the potato in the woman's hand. She closed her small fingers around it. She bowed at the waist to thank him and scurried off with her child. Once she had gone from him, his gaze became murderous and he locked in on the boy who had taken the food. He was standing, scraping the last of his tin into his mouth with his fingers. Daku gripped his heavy tin like one would a thick glass table ashtray, and approached him.

Without a word he slammed his tin across the boy's nose with enough force to crush it. Blood spewed out like hot ketchup. The boy cried out in agonizing pain. Tears burned his eyes as he tried to find and focus in on his assailant.

"FIGHT! FIGHT! FIGHT!" the group of men surrounding them chanted in their native language. The boy with the bloody nose was pushed in his back by some of the men, forcing him to engage. Daku took a few steps back and showed his teeth like a rabid wolf, flexing his muscles by rotating his shoulders and pumping his fist. The older, taller teenage boy tried to look down on Daku for show to his peers, but in his heart, he was scared shitless. The guards came running over to witness the action. One of them had two German Shepherds, which made the men open the circle to give them room. Immediately they began to bet.

The teen charged Daku with open arms, hoping to grab hold of him, but Daku side stepped him and gave him two bone-crushing blows to the ribs. The blows were so hard that the faces of the men surrounding them twisted in disfigurement as if they themselves had been struck. The boy fell to the ground, only to be picked up by the crowd and tossed back into action. This time the boy got lucky enough to land a blow to Daku's jaw. The boy, in awe of landing one, celebrated. Daku took the blow like a G and was so pissed that he growled like a wolf and showed his teeth again. This terrified the boy and he began to look for a means to escape. Daku tightened his fist and glared at his prey, thirsty for blood.

He took off in his direction at full speed and speared him so hard that his world went blank. A gunshot cracked the air and two guards broke up the fight. Not good for the teen boy though because the guard with the K9s bet his prostitute allowance that the boy would win and he didn't.

Daku was lying on his back in his bunk, staring off into nothingness when a guard came in to get him. "You," he said, pointing his gun. "Get up." Daku raised up and threw his legs over the side of his bunk. "Let's go." The guard led the way.

They crossed the dark grounds of the compound and went up a ramp and into what Daku knew was the General's hut. A guard stood on either side of the entrance, each holding an AK when they made it through the hut's opening. The General sat behind an unkempt wooden desk playing with a butterfly knife when his guest came through the doorway. His booted feet were propped up on the corner of his desk beside a fruit bowl. He took them down and closed his knife in one fancy motion. Behind him another guard stood in the fading moonlight coming through a window with a K9. It took everything in Daku to restrain himself to not go over and break the man's neck for what he'd done. The General recognized the murderous eyes of the youngster and smirked.

The aggression he witnessed fuming off the boy perversely impressed him. He sat the knife down in front of him then clasped his fingers behind it on his desk.

"Do you know why I brought you 'ere?" the General asked Daku.

Daku didn't answer but kept his eyes on the soldier in the back. The General stood and came around to the front of his desk where he rested his butt. "I find myself wondering where you learned to fight the way you do."

Daku was too naïve to know that he should've concealed his hatred for the soldier and continued to let his ruthless gaze rest on him. The General noticed this and decided to revise his line of questioning. Looking between the two of them with a sneer creasing the corner of his mouth, he smiled and said, "So, what is it that you want? What can I do for you?"

Daku pointed at the soldier. The General stood again, this time pacing the hut with his arms behind his back like Morpheus in the movie The Matrix. The smile never left his face. "So, you want a piece of my soldier, yes?" Daku nodded. The midnight black soldier with pink lips and gashes in his face just laughed.

"Let's say I give you this, and you manage to ki—"

"I bleed the ground with this child," the soldier cut in.

The General put a hand up to hush the soldier then stood in front of Daku with his arms once again behind his back.

"If you did manage to kill my soldier, who would replace him? The man you want a piece of is my sister's boy. What do I have to gain from this?"

For the first time since walking through the opening of the General's hut, Daku looked at him. Speaking with defiance he said, "My loyalty and my life for one I take."

Impressed by his answer, the General ordered everyone out to the open compound. Knowing that his nephew was skilled with a machete, he showed favor and arranged for them to fight with the weapons.

The morning air was cool and damp. The sun was just beginning to peek over the mountains in the backdrop. Guards and mineworkers formed a circle around the two gladiators. Two machetes were thrown on the muddy soil between them and the crowd erupted. Bets were made, most in favor of the soldier because he was older and they had seen him put in work before.

The two circled one another, feeling each other out. The soldier wore an over-confident smile since he'd seen many days inside this type of arena. He flinched at the machetes to make Daku think he was going for them. To his surprise, Daku was unfazed. This made him think twice about taking the fight too lightly with his adolescent opponent. *This boy has a fighter's spirit*, the soldier thought, and he dove to get his machete. He rolled to his feet and came down full force with the blade. Amazingly, Daku was swift and dived at his weapon, retrieving it just in time to block the soldier's blade as it came down the center of his face when the soldier brought his machete down.

Daku rolled to his left and quickly got to his feet. The crowd went wild at the two men's gladiatorial display. The soldier nodded at Daku, giving him props for the block and getting to his feet to at least give him some type of fight. But Daku didn't want his props. He wanted his head.

The soldier rotated his shoulders to loosen up.

"You may have the heart boy, but do you have the skills?" he asked mockingly. He then took off at Daku, swinging his blade wildly, not really trying to kill him, because he knew that Daku would block his careless onslaught. The soldier was putting on a show for the crowd and trying to wear him down with intimidation. Daku backed up into the crowd while blocking everything the soldier gave him. He watched the soldier wave his hands in the air to get the crowd hyped up, like a trained circus monkey. The solider twirled his machete with some impressive finger work. Daku recklessly went on the offensive, but the soldier seemed to know every uncalculated move the youngster came at him with. Daku didn't have a strategy and the advantage was clearly not his.

The soldier's confidence grew and he became tired of the games. He wanted to see blood. He decided he would kill Daku, but slowly. The solider swung his blade with more force, almost knocking Daku's from his hand. Catching Daku off guard and the solider landed a hard left to his jaw. It was as if he were fighting someone new. Before his mind could readjust, the soldier swung his blade again. Daku swayed back as the solider slashed him across the chest and stomach. Before he knew it, the blade was coming at him again and caught him across the right shoulder.

"Aaarrgh!" he screamed out. The crowd was going ballistic as the blade came back at Daku again. He tried helplessly to block it, but this time the soldier had his sights set on Daku's thigh. He gruesomely gashed his mark. Daku screamed out in pain and dropped to one knee, poising himself upright with the machete stuck in the mud. The burning sensation of the cuts was agonizing. Tears filled his eyes. He felt weak while the soldier fed off the energy of the crowd and seemed to get more skilled and stronger.

"KILL! KILL! KILL!" the crowd started to chant. They didn't give a fuck about Daku being a kid, because to them, he became a man the moment he put on boots too big for him.

Daku saw his life flash before him. Granny TuTu, Rahmi, Kenji, and Shassy. He'd seen the lives they lived and shared, then he saw it taken away from them, Kenji's and Shassy's right in front of him. Daku roared like a defeated lion, he became enraged. At that very moment, he refused to die. With revenge in his heart, Daku began to feed himself pure adrenaline. The soldier was feeling himself too much to know that his opponent was far from giving in to the deathblow he was intending to end his life with.

He charged Daku and swung his blade fiercely. Daku got to his feet. This stunned the soldier, who had to adjust his mark mid strike. Daku would capitalize on the mistake once again of his opponent celebrating too early. Daku swung his blade at the soldier's machete handle and cut off the soldier's fingers. In shock, the soldier's eyes followed his blade and fingers to the soft bloodstained mud. The transition from victor to victim apparently had a deadening effect to a warrior's judgment because the soldier's mind betrayed the number one rule in fighting; never take your eyes off your enemy.

His first lesson in why would be his last because Daku was swinging his blade again. Before the soldier could protest, Daku had found his mark. He planted the blade in the soldier's head like an axe in a tree. Daku snatched it out and replanted it before the soldier's body hit the ground.

Daku had silenced the cheering crowd, who only moments earlier thought it would be his blood spilling over the mud. The General smiled pleasantly and walked away with his arms folded behind his back. Daku stood over the soldier and spat on him with hatred.

"That's for Kenji!" He snatched the machete out of the soldier's head and chopped him between the legs barbarically. "And that's for my Shassy!" He spat on him again.

CHAPTER 5

Next to the Waldorf the Mickey Fleetwood Hotel Spa Resort was the next largest wonder in the world. It was located on Francis Beach. Like Chicago is to Harvey, Dolton, and Robins, just to name a few, Francis is to the Flux, Glory, and NuNu. Salomon stood in front of the full-length mirror on the door of his walk-in closet in his Anastasia suit, pushing the knot of his black Ralph Lauren tie towards his Adams apple. One of his partners sat on the plush king sized bed in a navy blue sweat suit with a white towel around his neck, tossing up an orange. He'd just left the spa and decided to stop in to have a few words with him, but after seeing his friend getting dapper, he now wondered where he was headed.

In his deep African accent he asked, "So, who iz deez loc-e damsel?"

Salomon turned from the mirror.

"How do I look?"

His partner Luis stopped playing catch with the orange and said, "Like a damn fool in dat Amurican garb."

"Flattery will get you everywhere my long time fwiend. Especially in dat sweat suit."

"Whooz de gurl?" Luis smiled. Out of all the partners who came along for the trip, these two were the closest.

Salomon went to the nightstand to pump on some Grey Flannel cologne. "She is de gal mi meet de udder night at de club."

"You caun't be serious, she is damaged goods. Not good enough for you. What con one see in a woman like dat?"

"Our nest egg. Dat gurl will lead us to Shaka and to us buying the lad out with mere dimes. We will have a beegar share in de mines which will mean more money for our families."

Luis rose from the bed and put a firm hand on Salomon's shoulder. "My fwiend, I like de sound of dat. I just hope you don't get cock whipped and stretch deez ordeal out longer than need be."

"When you compare a few million dollars to four diamond mines wort' billions," he put a hand on Luis's shoulder now, "my fwiend, what's a week or two?"

"Den it's settled," Luis gleamed. "Mi and de partners will leave you to deal wit dis peasant Shaka while we go to de west coast to check on our 'eroine business."

"Two weeks?"

"Yes," Luis said, leaving Salomon alone in his suite to think greedily about having Nikki in the room by himself for two whole weeks to do to her as he pleased.

"You look absolutely amazing," Salomon complimented Nikki as he held the door of the white stretch Hummer open for her to step in.

The night was warm so she decided on a lavender Prada body dress that fell just below her heart shaped ass. Her feet were adorned with bone white Gucci six-inch sandals and her hair was pinned up in a beautiful updo that let curls fall in the back like a Latin dance queen on Dancing with the Stars. Silver dust glistened on her shoulders and cleavage. She accented her style with diamond earrings, a pearl necklace and bracelet, and a white Ralph Lauren clutch with rhinestones.

"Hope I'm not over dressed," she giggled.

"Mi tink not. 'Ave you ever bean to ah ballet, no?"

"No. Not ever."

Salomon got in behind Nikki, admiring her ass-sets as he closed the door behind him. "Well, dis is not your teepicall ballet. De t'eme is Gangstas Need Luv 2. You'll love it. It's a Reggie Brown production, 'ave you 'eard of 'im?"

"I'm not sure that I have, but I'll trust your judgment," she said, having a seat as she took in the luxuries of the Hummer limo. She crossed her long legs high to give Salomon an eye full of her neatly shaved pussy. Unknown to her, he'd already gotten a full view of everything as he got in the limo behind her.

"Mi tink mi can oblige," he said, seated across from her trying to disguise his hard-on with some smooth leg crossing of his own. He was seated next to the crystal bar aligning the wall.

"That's nice," she commented, noticing the lights dance off the glass.

He looked. "Mi tink so too."

Nikki was impressed by how graceful Salomon handled the bar. Even the way he took the wine flutes between his fingers and poured them a drink from the Dom bottle. She accepted the drink from him with delicate fingertips. "Thank you."

"You're welcomb," he said, lifting his glass. "A toast."

Nikki held her glass close to her chest and asked skeptically, "A toast to what? You haven't had me to yourself but a few minutes."

Salomon gave a sly smile. "Den lets toast to the few minutes."

"To a few minutes," Nikki chimed in brilliantly, then clanked glasses with him.

"Salute!"

The two left the theater hand in hand as the stretch Hummer pulled up to greet them at the end of the red carpet. "Did you enjoy de show?" he asked politely.

"Men in tights flying through the air like birds bussin' they straps to classical music and shit. Who woulda ever thought that some fairy ass niggaz could get gangstafied," Nikki said and laughed at her own witty banter.

"So mi take it dat you liked it, yes?" At this time the chauffer was around the Hummer to open the door for them.

Stepping in Nikki answered, "I must admit, I did. Although, honestly, I didn't think I would." Salomon got in behind her, deeply inhaling Nikki's womanly fragrances and getting a massive hard-on again.

"Well that's good. Are you 'ungry?"

"Starved," she answered, going into her clutch to retrieve an already rolled blunt. "Do you mind?" she asked him with the blunt between her fingertips.

He took the blunt from her and smelled the vanilla leaf the pine cess was wrapped in.

"Not at all," he exhaled, then took the Zippo from his jacket pocket and fired the blunt up. Nikki was in awe and chuckled femininely.

"I never would've taken you to smoke weed."

"Gunja."

A thick cloud escaped his mouth and he chased it all down. "Not since mi college days."

"Looks to me like you still got it. You go boy."

They finished the blunt on the way to the hotel. They agreed to order room service and chill in his suite with the television. Nikki had planned on going back there with him even before they discussed it, because she wanted to tease him into staying a couple of weeks or more. If she were a crystal ball reader, she'd have already known he'd taken care of the trouble her and Mika faced concerning time. The only thing left to do was left up to Mika.

They dined on muscles in fish curry and cream, fried clams, garlic buttered lobster tails, fluffy cheddar biscuits, steamed broccoli, and potatoes baked in olive oil smothered in sour cream and chives. Salomon wiped the corners of Nikki's mouth after feeding her the meal with his fingers. And she made sure she sucked them clean seductively.

"So, what are your plans?" she asked him with her feet over his lap as she sat with her back comfortably perched on the inner arm of the plush sofa.

Salomon had started to massage and plant tiny kisses on her bare feet. He loved how pretty and soft they were. "What do you mean?" he asked huskily, really starting to work her feet over with the balls of his thumbs.

She moaned. "I mean, how long are you in town?"

"I 'ave two weeks to find Shaka and get 'im to sign de papers we 'ave for 'im, den mi and my people con leave."

Surprised that she didn't have to coax him into staying by keeping her pussy on lock playing games made her wet, and she could tell that Salomon was just as excited because his dick was harder than Chinese arithmetic pressing against the back of her calves, pulsating.

"So where are your peeps now?"

"Oh, dey 'eaded to de west coast to tend to udder bizness."

Pussy on fire and needing to put the flames out, Nikki intended to play with the information Salomon was in search of until Mika positioned herself properly in her plan. Until then, Salomon could beat her back out for bits and pieces. "Hey Salomon," she moaned.

"Yes, pussycat?"

"Do you eat pussy?"

Caught off guard, he looked Nikki in the eyes and said, "Mi eat pussy like mi been raised on goat teats."

Nikki raised up on her elbows. "Huh?"

Salomon smiled brightly. "Lay bahk. Mi show you what mi mean..."

CHAPTER 6

Nikki was still in awe of all the food and the smells that were making her anxious to dive in. "Straight black."

Salomon smiled and poured her a mug. "Look at all this food," she said, tasting the fish for starters. It melted in her mouth like butter. Her eyes rolled to the back of her head. Her taste buds were in heaven. "Mmm..."

He sat the coffee mug on her table. "I take it dat you like de food," he chuckled, appreciating her child-like ways.

"It's amazing," she giggled, and forked up some eggs chasing it with a bite of toast.

"Good. I'm going to take a shower now."

With her mouth full she said, "What about all this food?"

He leaned over and kissed her forehead. "I'll eat some in a bit. I wanna shower first."

She drank some juice with both her hands around the glass like a fat kid in the hood that greedily wanted to wash down his food. She burped. "Are you trying to fatten me up?" she asked after wiping her mouth with the back of her hand.

Salomon couldn't help but let out a genuine laugh. "No," he said and headed for the bathroom where he dropped his Calvin Klein boxers at the door so that she could admire his naked body. She almost choked on her juice from the sight of him standing ass naked in the light, then mumbled something under her breath when she recovered.

"What waz dat?" he asked over his shoulder, letting her know he'd heard her. He then flexed his back muscles and hardened his shiny, sculpted ass cheeks for effect.

"Nothing," she mouthed, admiring the view.

"I'll be out in a minute," he teased, closing the door to a crack.

Nikki picked up the remote to turn on the forty-two-inch television mounted on the wall. She channel surfed through the stations and stopped when she saw an anvil fall from the sky and bash Wile E. Coyote on the head. She hadn't enjoyed breakfast in bed and cartoons since she was a kid and took advantage of the opportunity to just chill like a kid again. But like any wet dream, something always messes it up. Her phone rang. When Nikki saw that it was Mika, she quickly accepted.

"I was just about to call you, bitch," she lied, although she had planned to, just not at that very moment.

"What up? Did you forget that you were supposed to gimme an immediate yes or no on the two-week deal? You know visitation at the jail is at eleven."

Nikki dropped her fork on the plate and sat it on the table on the other side of the bed. She threw her legs over the side to sit up and talk.

"Damn girl, I forgot how they be doing shit at them damn jails."

"Fuck all that, did you get the time or not?"

"You know your girl..."

Mika hung up, leaving Nikki looking at a blank screen and listening to the dial tone. She was in a hurry to leave the house. She wanted to make it to the jail before eleven. Otherwise, she would have to wait until one o'clock and she didn't want to do all that waiting in no stuffy ass jail in no hot ass tailored maternity clothes with a makeshift six-month silicone belly and swollen titties body suit underneath. She grabbed her keys off the kitchen table and shot out the door.

Mika went over her game plan for what seemed like the thousandth time on her ride to the jail, and although she hadn't seen or talked to Shaka in six months, she knew he'd be happy to see her. Why wouldn't he be? She was pregnant with his seed. A son...Shaka Jr. She smiled. "It's true, Tiara, I am a bitch," she said laughing.

*****

Pulling up to the tri county jail, she killed the engine. Mika checked her makeup and teeth for plum colored lipstick stains in the rearview mirror before stepping out. When her silver Giuseppe Zanotti flats touched the gravel lot, she stood and slid her L's in the back pocket of her Junya Wantanabe jeans. Mika knew that even in her dress down gear she was the baddest bitch about to grace the county jail. And that was her intention; to show Shaka she was that even when she wasn't trying to be, pregnant and all. She closed her Audi door and stepped across the lot to the side entrance.

Upon entering the jail, Mika had to sign the waiting list with the officer who sat behind a cheap ass desk reading a Stuff magazine. To her surprise there were only a few people scattered about waiting to see their loved ones, so getting back to see Shaka should happen without delay. She picked up the pen to sign in to see Bryce Vaughn, the name Shaka's adoptive parents had given him as a baby when they were put in the position to take care of him.

*****

Shaka stumbled across his birth certificate in a blank envelope at the bottom of his mother's leather treasure chest that looked like a trunk. When he saw that his mother's name on the birth certificate was Leah with no last name, and that he was born in Tanzania, South Africa, he questioned his parents about his discovery.

Holding his evidence up for them to see, he asked, "Who am I?"

His mother Ciara's eyes welled up and spilled over as she went to him. "Oh baby, I'm so sorry," she said, reaching out to console him.

Shaka shook from her embrace. Ciara's heart sank immediately. Shaka felt as if he were living a lie and the people in front of him were sixteen years' worth of phony.

"Son," his father Marcus said in a pleading tone.

"Let's all sit down and talk about this after dinner."

"Fuck that! I've been..."

"Bryce?" his mother said. She had not raised him to be vulgar.

"You will not use that tone in my home," his father roared.

"Apologize to your mother, NOW!"

"She's not my mother," he said to hurt them, because at that moment, he felt betrayed by the world. "Why you ungrateful..." Marcus began, stepping to Bryce.

But Bryce held up the .22 caliber pistol that he found in the chest beside the old lady's bible and put a stop to Marcus's advance.

"All I asked you people was who I am and you gonna step to me?" His eyes were watering but untamed.

"I'm the one who has been lied to. I'm the only one in this house who don't know who he is. Y'all laid up being husband and wife playing house and shit, like I was a live-in Cabbage

Patch. I wanna know who made y'all God?" He cocked the hammer back. "You think you God, dawg?"

"Please, Bryce. Please, just stop," Ciara begged with her hands clasped as if in prayer. "You shouldn't be mad at us for doing our best with you. Your mother sent you to us so that you could live. All we did was raise you as our own."

He kept the gun aimed at Marcus's chest. "So I woulda died had she kept me?"

"You have to believe..."

"I don't have to believe shit. After all the lies, how could either of y'all ask a nigga to believe?"

"Well Bryce, you know it all," Marcus said. "Now what you gone do with that gun?"

He lowered the gun. "According to this paper right here," he held up the paper, "I'm Shaka Keymundu and," he tossed the papers at Marcus, making them rain to the floor, "you people can kiss my ass." That was the last time Shaka had talked to the people who had raised him. Ciara was ordered by Marcus not to ever reach out to help Shaka, or ever speak of his name again. And though her heart yearned for her to go to him, she would honor her husband's wishes.

*****

Years had gone by and she never once let his name pass her lips.

When Shaka moved away from Miami to the Flux, he only shared that part of his life with Mika, which is why she knew his government name. Nevertheless, when she signed in to see Bryce Vaughn, she saw another woman was there to see her man.

"Who the fuck is Kiana Jackson?"

"That's me."

Mika thought she'd asked the question under her breath until this lil Aaliyah looking chic answered. Humph, Mika grunted, and rolled her eyes at the youngster whose sense of style were Guess Jeans, a calendar shirt, and pink Chuck Taylors.

A group of people exited from the back while the next group prepared to go. Mika was fuming walking beside the Kiana girl, but she sucked it up and figured she'd play her cards right with Shaka, using the girl as a pawn to make him uncomfortable and guilt stricken.

Mika made small talk with Kiana while Shaka was being brought from the cellblock. There was only room for one of them to sit on the metal stool placed in front of the Plexiglas and blue phone booth style visiting area, so Mika told Kiana that she could have the seat because she'd rather stand. She had planned on Shaka coming out as he normally did to visit his guest and then be shocked when he saw her in the background playing the wall, all swollen up. Kiana told Mika that she had just recently started coming to see Shaka and that she was his homeboy Rydah's little sister. It only made sense that Kiana came to see him because Rydah was the only nigga Shaka would trust to know his government name. But Rydah wasn't about to visit no nigga in jail, homeboy or not, so he used Kiana to pass messages and put money on his books, which she was more than willing to do because she'd had a crush on him since she was a pup.

To Mika, she still was. The only thing that made her a smart pup was the fact that she at least went after someone that high social standings in the hood. *You go gurl*, Mika thought, because little do you know you was about to be fuckin' with a multi-millionaire, just not today. Mika rubbed her belly, thinking and smiling about how she was about to come up.

The door opened on the other side of the Plexiglas and inmates were starting to filter through to their loved ones. Mika and Kiana were in the last booth so Shaka made it in last in accordance with placement. He started smiling proudly when he saw Kiana, with her pretty self, waiting on the stool with the phone to her ear anxious to see and talk to him. He picked up the phone before he took his seat. Then out of nowhere, his happy expression turned murderous and Kiana began to wonder what the fuck just happened and what the fuck she had just gotten caught in the middle of.

"Is everything aiight with you?" Kiana asked him. She wasn't comfortable enough with Mika to look back and assess how she was responding to the blood in Shaka's expression.

His jaw clenched tight. His forearm muscles rippled and his grip on the phone made his bronze knuckles turn white. If looks could kill, Mika would've been body bagged.

"Yeah, I'm good," he seethed. But Shaka wasn't trying to mask his true emotions with what he knew Kiana wanted to hear just to ease her worry. His mind had instantaneously shot back to the night he got popped only to let Mika get away, and his mouth was just going through the motions on autopilot. In his mind, he still had the caper mapped out perfectly and nothing could go wrong.

*****

"Nothing will go wrong if you just listen to me," he told Mika reassuringly. "Just before you get in the car with the nigga, call me and put the phone in your pocket. That way I can hear everything that's goin' on and can find you with the family locator app, feel me?"

"Why can't you just follow us?" Mika asked Shaka as she applied her MAC products in the visor mirrors with the lights turned on the sides.

"Because that country nigga Slow ain't slow. He gone be lookin' for some ill shit. Think about it, three ma'fuckas in his clique been deaded, so we gotta be smart when it comes to this chumo. There's a reason he's the last one standing out here in these streets. And what nigga don't know the quickest way to wake up dead is to fall asleep in some pussy?"

Mika flipped the visor back up and turned to Shaka. "I feel you, but I'd just feel better if you were closer than tracking me by phone."

"I'll only be five minutes behind you. So, by the time y'all get out the ride, I'll be pullin' in wherever y'all at." Shaka cocked his gun in the air and put one in the chamber of his chrome .45. "You just get that nigga away from his iron."

Mika opened the Tahoe door to let herself out. "Don't you worry about that," she said as she patted her clutch. "I got that nigga if shit goes south." Little did she know that the law of attraction was in full affect with the full moon that night, and she would have to stand on that slick shit she was popping.

Mika got out of the cab on 39th and DeeDee where Slow said he would be waiting for her at the corner. He was three blocks away watching her through binoculars when she exited the Yellow cab. When he saw her pull out the phone he retrieved his from the passenger seat of his maroon 2012 Lincoln MKX. Just as he suspected, she called him.

"Hey, where are you?" she crooned.

"Coming up the block now... I see you." Mika turned just in time to see Slow pull away from the curb a few blocks away.

Immediately she knew that he was watching her to make sure she traveled alone. *Hmmm, Shaka might know a lil somethin' somethin'*, she thought with a smile. "So how you gone have a bad bitch like me standing out here on a corner like I'm some kinda bust down because you late?"

"I'm not late, baby girl. You just early," he joked.

This bitch ass nigga trying to play a bitch like I'm desperate. "Oh really?"

"Yeah. And I bet after tonight when Slow put his thang down on you that you gone be callin' ole Slow for booty calls like he the bust down. So, all's fair when you consider that into my being late as you say."

"I'm not impressed," Mika said. "Normally when a nigga do all that jive ass rappin', he just trying to let that slick shit compensate for a small dick," she laughed.

"Don't tell me ole Slow fallin' a lil shawty tween the legs," she said, holding her hand up so he could see her index finger come to within an inch of her thumb.

By this time Slow was pulled over in front of Mika pushing his passenger door open. "I see you got jokes."

Mika rolled her neck. "I see you do too," she sassed.

"What?"

"You better get out that car and come open my door."

Slow threw the car in park. "Aw man, you gone make ole Slow get out fa'real, huh?"

"Ya think." Mika closed the passenger door and folded her arms over her breast.

Shaka was close behind listening to the whole scenario on three-way. Slow was on the other side of his car opening the door for Mika.

"At your service, playa."

"Don't get jazzy," she said, smiling while taking her seat, placing the live phone in her jacket pocket. The slowly drove in circles for the first ten minutes of their ride looking for any signs of a tail. Once he was satisfied there weren't any, he drove to the next town over, which was Glory. There he found a nice restaurant and pulled in.

"What you know about the Soul Le' Front?" Mika teased.

"You must thank ole Slow ain't got no class, huh?" Mika blushed. Slow appreciated the warmth of it and opened his car door.

"Come on. Let's go in."

"You better get over here and open my door, Mr. I ain't got no...," she sassed when his door was closing. The maître d' ushered them to a red leather booth in the rear of the restaurant lit up by electric candles stationed on two sides of the round table. He placed their menus in front of them. "Your waiter will be with you momentarily. May I interest you in a drink? I hear the Moscato is a great opener," he said politely, and winked as

55

he whispered, "The Barefoot is my favorite followed by some Dom P."

"Then send us both bottles over," Mika chimed in.

"Chilled my man," Slow added.

"Fine." The maître d' wrote something on his pad. "Coming right up. You two have a beautiful evening and if there's anything I can do for you, please don't hesitate to let me know."

"Thank you," Mika said.

"You're welcome. Thanks for choosing Soul Le' Front," he replied, and walked away with a broad smile and a slight sway in his hips.

"That boy gay as a two dolla bill," Slow said.

Mika hit him on the shoulder playfully and laughed. "Boy, you a fool."

"He is. Shit." Slow slid out of the booth. "I gotta go take a piss. My bladder can't take no mo'." And here I was giving ole Slow some credit for having some class.

As soon as Slow bent the corner to take a piss, Mika pulled out her phone and spoke into it.

"Where you at?"

"I'm right outside," Shaka said.

"Fuck is this nigga on with this ole wining and dining you shit?"

"You should take some pointers. Just like a nigga, wanna fuck somethin' fye but don't wanna do all that fye shit that come wit it."

"Whateva. I done paid to play already."

"And that's the problem. You done got too comfortable. If I close these ma'fuckin legs, I bet you get some act right."

"Yeah right. See, the thing is, I know you like it rough, so all I'ma do is take it because I know that's all you want a nigga to do anyway."

"Boy, shut up," she chuckled. "You kill me."

Shaka laughed. "Trying to kill that ma'fucka, ya feel me? And look, make that nigga comfortable. Get him to talkin' so we can know where that safe at before I dead his ass."

"Come on now, you talkin' like a bitch slow," she said, laughing at her own pun.

"I'm fa'real, Mika. Keep that nigga talkin'."

"I got you. Up...Uh oh, gotta go," she said, sticking the phone in her jacket pocket again then taking the jacket off and placing it on the side of her as Slow made his way back to the table. Slow sat down. "As fancy as this place is they still ain't brought the dranks over to the table yet."

"Here it comes now," Mika informed him, looking over his shoulder.

Slow undid another button on his wine-colored silk Versace shirt. "Good, I'm ready to loosen up. I been tight all day. You?"

"Not so much."

The waiter sat the ice buckets down with their drink choices in them on the edge of the table then placed a wine glass with a gold rim in front of each of them. After filling their glasses, he took their orders. "I'll have the lobster stuffed steak with garlic mashed potatoes, broccoli, grilled shrimp with lemon, and cheddar biscuits." The waiter wrote on his pad. "And for the lady?" he asked, looking at Mika.

Slow cut in, "Oh she'll be having the same."

The waiter looked at Slow then back to Mika for confirmation. She put a hand on her chest as if what Slow had just done took her breath away. "I guess I am," she replied breathlessly.

"Excellent choices. My name is Michael and I'll be back shortly. Enjoy your drinks."

The take-charge attitude Slow had just displayed turned Mika's pussy medium rare. *If he keeps this up...*she twitched in her seat. *Too bad he gotta die.* Mika didn't find chubby niggaz attractive, but Slow had a healthy bankroll. She made herself find somebody famous to compare him to just to keep her from running. He had lips like Twista with KRS-1 and dressed like foine ass Morris Chestnut. She smiled, *that's gonna have to do.*

"You didn't like me ordering for you?" Slow asked.

Mika's brows came together as if she were deeply concerned or in thought. "Nah. Just kinda threw me off."

"I hope in a good way."

"Actually, yes."

"Well, good." He downed his glass then filled it again.

They chopped it up like old friends through dinner and all the way back to the car. Slow started the motor.

"You know, I feel like I've known you all my life. I'm actually comfortable around you."

"Really?" Mika was taken aback. "I didn't think that was possible on a first date."

"Well it is." He turned his lights on and pulled out.

"I have a room at the Mickey Fleetwood Spa Resort, you trying to go? I don't want you feelin' like I was doing all this to bed you, first off. Secondly, I need to smoke some good good. And lastly, I'm actually looking forward to calling you tomorrow to talk to you for hours about nothing in particular." Slow was saying all the right shit.

I might have to mercy fuck this nigga his last night on Earth. "That's some soft ass shit, Slow. Yeah, we can go to your room to smoke."

"Believe me, Mika, ain't nothin' soft 'bout Slow. I can show you better than I can tell you. Now, how about that smoke?"

"Sounds to me like more compensation talk."

"Humph," Slow snickered, followed by a sly grin. "You gone see."

They took a quiet elevator ride up to the sixteenth floor where Slow had booked his suite. As soon as they got in the room, Slow grabbed Mika by the throat and threw her into the wall, knocking all the wind out of her lungs. He then covered her mouth with his.

Mika was in shock and didn't know how to respond to what Slow was doing to her. At first, she thought he was about to fuck her up. She started fumbling with her clutch to retrieve her pistol, but then he was kissing her hard and passionately. Not only that, but his hand slid under her skirt and his fingers had expertly moved her thong over and he was finger fucking her. *What the fuck*, she thought. Slow sucked her bottom lip then pulled away.

"You like that?"

Mika was at a loss for words but managed to nod her head. Slowly he took his finger out of her and put his arms firmly around her waist then started dry humping her. Mika could feel his large dick on her leg and regretted that compensation shit she shot at him earlier.

"Hold on," Mika said breathlessly. She tried to pull back. Slow gritted then turned her in his arms and forced her over the chair.

"Wait a minute..." Slow wasn't trying to hear her. He pushed her skirt up and over her rounded ass cheeks and somehow had his pants puddled around his ankles with the

60

swiftness. He held her thong to the side and was dick head first in her pussy hole so fast it scared her. She did her best to keep her moans shush because she knew that Shaka could hear everything that was going on.

"Let me...take...uuh...take my j-jacket off...ew shit...and put it...oww...on...on the bed. Oh shit. Eww wee...goddamn." She wanted desperately to muffle the phone.

"Fuck that shit." He slapped her ass and continued to thrust himself deeper and deeper into her wetness. "I'm not coming...up...out...this pussy. I'ma make this my...shit."

Mika tried her best to conceal her escapade with Slow, but the more he fucked her from the back, the better his dick got and it seemed to grow, and before Mika knew what was taking over her, she was throwing the pussy back at him.

"Goddamn, daddy...you...fuckin' the shit outta me."

This wasn't the first time Shaka had gotten an earful of Mika fuckin' another dude, so that wasn't the bother. What got him teed was the fact that she wasn't controlling the situation like she did with the others and this had him fuming. He needed her to get Slow away from his gun and for her to give him the green light to bum rush the spot. He had all the info he needed to hit Slow's trap spots to recover his riches. Now all he had to do was dead Slow like he did his men.

"This bitch act like she enjoying the shit," he said, taking in the fuck session like a G.

Slow felt his nut coming on strong and pumped Mika's wet pussy harder. She moaned and groaned with great pleasure. She admitted to herself that Slow was a dick throwing beast and let her guard down to enjoy being fucked silly.

Slow couldn't hold on any longer and pulled out. He shot his hot load on Mika's back, messing up her shirt and skirt with his nut.

"Wow!" he said, smearing the last of his juices on her ass. Too caught up in the moment, she didn't realize what he did to her clothes. She was spent and still bent over the chair trying to catch her breath.

"Oh shit!" Slow said, pulling his pants up.

"What?"

"We gotta go!"

"What?"

"Hurry up. We gotta go now!"

Mika adjusted her clothes. Slow took her arm and rushed them out the door. They hurriedly made it through the lobby. Once by the exit Slow said, "Oh shit, I forgot something in the room. Wait one second. Don't move!" He bent the corner out of sight and as soon as he did, Mika got on her phone.

"We getting' ready to come out."

"I can see you standing by the exit from here, but where he dip off to?"

"He went back to the room."

"What the fuck you mean he went back to the room? I told you, you gotta stay on that nigga."

"That nigga don't have a clue what we on so chill," she said, hoping to reassure Shaka.

"Sounded like you didn't have a clue while he was... hold on..." Something had Shaka's attention. "Yo, blue and red cherries comin' straight at your side of the building and them desk bitches is moving behind you."

"Damn straight, bitch ass nigga," Slow cut in.

"Yo dumb ass bitch never cut her three-way off. I hope she like jail cause that's where she goin' wit that pistol in her clutch trying to stick up the resort." Mika's heart fell in her thong. She knew that Slow must've been listening to them talk when he went to take a piss at the restaurant. How else could he have known? That's how he knew to force himself... She felt so used, stupid, and careless. "I'ma kill you, ma'fucka," she said, deathly serious.

"Yeah, yeah," Slow mocked then hung up.

"Fuck that, right now run for the other door!" Shaka yelled into the phone then threw it on the other seat. He drove the Tahoe recklessly over the concrete divisions on the lot and through the shrubs inside them trying to get to Mika. Shots were fired in the direction of the police. They ducked inside their cruisers until the coast was clear, then took pursuit of the Tahoe that had just drove passed them wildly. When they

63

finally pulled the driver over, they smiled as one cop dangled the .45 he found under Shaka's seat with two fingers.

"Got 'em."

CHAPTER 7

They could not break the man they had tied buck ass naked to a chair. The rebels were beating him within inches of his life. Not with bats, canes, or stones as one would think. They were only using braided blades of cornhusk. What made the method of torture so effective were the thousands of army ants they had woven inside cloth-like sheets with their stinger ends facing the flesh of the man. They taped these sheets over the man's back, arms, stomach, thighs, and feet, and any time the sheets were hit with the braided corn husk, the ants would sting relentlessly in sync all over his body, using an attack pheromone to communicate, zapping him of all his strength and leaving him unable to fight back. He was sweating profusely from fever and delusion at this point.

He repeated the phrase, "I am Prince Bontana, ruler of the Swanabea Tribe," through the pain he was enduring. Just as he was repeating himself, Daku came through the opening of the large hut. "I am Prince Bontana, ruler of the Swanabea Tribe."

"And I am Daku, leader of the Rebel Army." A silence fell over the room. Finally, after what seemed like forever, but only a moment passed, Stone, Daku's right hand man and advisor, said, "He refuses to sign over his land to us."

Prince Bontana let out a funky laugh then coughed harshly. The entire room, which consisted of Daku, Stone and two other rebels, looked upon him.

"Daku, I've heard...stories...of you."

The two sideline rebels began to hit the sheets of pissed off ants with the braided husk. The prince shook violently. His flesh was extremely hot and swollen. His head lolled from side to side, defeated. Daku held his hand up for the rebels to stop.

"What stories have you heard about me?" Daku asked with a comedic drawl, wanting nothing more than to be entertained by the man's answer. He whispered something incoherently.

"What did you say?" One of the rebels was about to swing his husk.

"No," Daku ordered, and the rebel stopped mid-swing.

"I'll handle this." Daku walked over to Prince Bontana and put his ear close to his mouth.

"Repeat what you said for me." He whispered something again. This time Daku was able to make out what he said as a bewildered look etched across his face.

For the first time since he'd taken Daku under his wing, Stone witnessed panic glaze over his pupil's features. Daku rushed to take the sheets of ants from the man's body and untie him.

"Get this man into ice water, NOW! I swear to Allah, if he dies, you die!" he said to every man in the room.

CHAPTER 8

"So, we're approved?" Mika asked, waiting at the red light. The light turned green. She eased on the gas. "Yeah," Shaka answered as he stood at one of the two phones on the wall in his cellblock's dayroom while the other inmates sat at the metal tables slamming dominoes or playing dirty hearts. He put his shoulder on the wall then crossed his legs at the ankles.

"You know your boy got pull," he said.

Mika giggled. "Boy don't even act like you the shit right now." Shaka laughed. It felt good to feel whole again. "And all I have to do is come in with a signed marriage license and a preacher this weekend and we can get it done?" she asked.

"Basically, yea."

"So, when I'ma get my ring? I ain't takin' nothin' less than five karats my nigga."

"I wouldn't respect you if you did."

"Whatever, you full of shit." Mika came to life as soon as she heard her song begin to play on the radio. She started snapping her fingers as she turned it up.

"Don't you dare slow down, go longer, you can last more rounds, push harder, you almost there now, so go lover, make mama proud and when we're done, I don't wanna feel my legs..."

"That ma'fucka sound hard. Who sing that shit?" Shaka asked, bobbing his head.

"That's that Kelly Rowland and Lil Wayne joint, Motivation."

"Dat ma'fucka hard."

"Hell yeah," she agreed.

"Anyways, how's my baby?"

"Baby?"

"Yeah. Or did you forget you was pregnant?"

Caught up in the music moment, Mika almost forgot the fake pregnancy she'd created about carrying Shaka's shorty.

"Boy, I thought you was calling me baby, and I ain't been used to hearin' that shit is all. My fat ass better be pregnant."

"So how my boy doing? When yo next doctor's appointment?"

"He all good. I go to the doctor for ultra sounds again in a few weeks."

"I want pictures. Didn't you get some the first time?"

"Yeah."

"Send 'em."

"I gave 'em to Tiara because I wanted her to surprise me with the sex of the baby on a day I wasn't feelin' my best."

"Seems like I'm missing out on all the fuckin' moments dealin' with this jail shit."

"I'm sorry."

"Don't be. I'll be home soon."

"Boy what you know I don't know?" she asked sarcastically.

Mika knew those white folks wasn't about to let his black ass go any time soon. *Nigga you shot at the police,* is what she wanted to say over the phone, but kept it to herself. Shaka laughed. One way or the other he was getting outta jail.

"That's my fifteen minutes of fame," he said when the phone beeped. "I'ma call you tonight before lockdown."

"I'll be waitin' on it."

"Mika, I love you. I'm glad you came back to me with my son."

"Don't say shit like that, Shaka. You gone make a bitch cry."

"Later," he said. Then the line went dead. He hung the phone up and went to his room to smoke a joint.

"Yo, Messy," he called to one of the four men sitting at the gray painted metal picnic tables playing dirty hearts. When he looked up from just getting planted with the bitch (the queen of spades), Shaka asked, "You tryin' to get up on one or what?"

Messy immediately got to his feet. "Hell yeah!" he answered excitedly.

"Damn my nigga," another dude at the table said. "It's like that?"

Shaka turned and coolly said, "I ain't never fucked with you, Randy. So live yours my nigga."

* * * * *

Mika hung up her phone and began scolding herself for the slip up with that baby bullshit. To get her mind off things and to loosen up, she called Tiara.

"What's up, bitch?"

"What it is, Mika, Ms. M.I.A.?" Tiara teased. "Thought you forgot about lil ole me."

"Neva-dat-one. You know how I be gettin' busy out here in these necessary skreets."

"Well, I ain't heard from you in a month of Sundays. You musta done came up."

"Finna, bitch. What you got goin' right now?"

"Girl, lookin' at Mama in the mirror tryin' to fix her dry ass wig," Tiara laughed, looking at her mama struggle to get her wig right. "That shit crooked Mama."

"Well, GODDAMMIT, help me, shit!"

"Bitch you better help Ms. Lyday foe she have a muthafuckin' seizure or somethin'," Mika kidded in her Tupac voice. They laughed. "Anyways, I'm finna pick up Nikki's ass and then come and get you so we can ball at the mall. I'm needin' me some new gear, ya heard."

"Aiight, I'll be ready."

"Girl if you don't get off that phone and help me with this wig. I didn't spend thirty-five dollars on this damn thing to have Harold from the Butcher Block laughin' tonight," Ms. Lyday said, and then started mumbling. "Carried your lil ungrateful ass for nine whole months, got stretch marks on my stomach that make my shit look like a piece of balled up paper and you can't help me. Lil bitch, I bet if I snatch a knot in you fast ass...," she continued on.

"Okay Mama, dag, I get it, shoot," Tiara said to her mama then whispered into the phone, "Bitch, hurry up."

Her mama eavesdropped and said, "What you say?"

Mika pulled up to Tiara's crib and blew the horn. Tiara came out the house dressed in some rhinestone covered blue jean Capri pants, a pink halter top with a baby blue button up tied in a knot under her C-cup titties, and some icy-white Ones. Her hair was pulled back in a ponytail.

"Well, if we not just the cutest thing today," Mika teased as Tiara sat in the front seat of Mika's Audi.

"Where Nikki? I thought you was pickin' her up?" Tiara asked, closing the door.

Mika talked while backing out of the driveway.

"She had the nerve to conveniently accidentally hit the answer button when I called her and let me hear her getting her back knocked out."

"Hell to da naw," Tiara shook her head.

Mika laughed. "Ain't that some shit?" She hit her right blinker when she came to the stop sign at the end of street.

71

"Yep. And guess what"

"What?" Mika asked, making the turn.

"Yo boy Bogus tried to get at me when you quit answering his calls."

Mika took her eyes off the road to look at Tiara. "Straight?"

"Yep. Talkin' bout how y'all done and what's up with me?"

Mika turned her attention back to the road. "Niggaz and flies. The more I fuck wit niggaz, the more I like flies."

Tiara's brows furrowed. "Say that again," she asked. Mika obliged. "I like that. I'ma have to steal it." Mika hunched her shoulders. "Anyway, I told his ass to step. Knowin' yo ass, you prolly gave him herpes just to keep the dick on lock."

"Bitch I know you didn't just take it there."

"Yes I did. I should call that nigga up when I have another outbreak and have him eat me," Mika laughed.

"Eww...you laughin' but bitch, you know you ain't playin'." They pulled up to the Boddum 2 Da Top mall, found a spot in the back by the security entrance, and went inside.

"Well, lets hit up Foot Locker."

Mika rolled her eyes. "Foot Locker? Bitch iz you crazy?" She tossed her hair back with her hand. "You better go across the street with that shit," Mika sassed in her best Ice Cube in Boyz n the Hood impersonation.

"Well, since you're buying, where you wanna go?" Tiara shot back with a smile.

Mika laughed. "You know what to say, don't you?" She shook her head. "You know you somethin' else, right?"

"What, you ain't know?"

After going to a few stores and only coming out with a pair of Marc Jacob stilettos, Mika was ready to go. Tiara, on the other hand, had to run into Wet Seal to grab the Hollister halter top she had her eyes set on for the past week or so.

"You really have to have that ole white girl ass shirt, don't you?" Mika teased.

Tiara laughed. "And you know this man," impersonating Chris Tucker in Friday.

Mika laughed. "Hurry up, bitch. My hair startin' to frizz."

Tiara took an armful of clothing into the dressing room and put a couple pairs of pants and shirts on under her clothes and came out beaming as though she had only decided on her original choice, the halter-top. Mika was heated. She knew that Tiara's load was a little lighter and pulled her ass back into the dressing room. "What the fuck are you doing," Mika snapped.

"Damn, bitch, what you talking about?" Tiara shot back, trying to shake Mika.

"This!" Mika said, pulling at Tiara's pants and shirt. "I'm trying to get me a few extra things without having to pay for them. What's the big deal?"

"What's the big deal? *WHAT'S THE BIG DEAL?* Are you that ma'fuckin' stupid?" Mika snatched at Tiara's clothes. "Take it off!"

"Aiight, damn." Tiara felt bad as she peeled the clothes off.

"I was just trying to do something for myself like you do." She was crying a river now.

Mika could tell that Tiara was sincerely distraught over the situation. Nonetheless, she felt it was her moral obligation to keep Tiara on the straight and narrow. Kinda like her good deed to cover all the bad shit she did in life.

"Whatever you need Tiara, I'll buy. You don't have to steal shit. That's for them bird bitches, not bosses like us." Tiara handed Mika the items as embarrassment set in.

"I'm sorry, Mika. I mean it. I'm just trying to come into my own."

Mika took Tiara into her motherly arms. They hugged the pain away then came apart.

"Tiara, I got you. You my lil sister and if I have to rob every nigga in the Flux to keep you outta the bullshit, then that's what's up."

"Heeey, Tiara a pimp," she sang, breaking the tension.

"Don't push it, bitch," Mika laughed.

"Sorry."

"Now let's get up outta here foe I have to snap on these white folks up in here." Mika paid for the gear Tiara wanted and they headed out the mall.

"Well, well..." Kiana said, seeing Mika and Tiara leaving the mall. Mika didn't have her fake pregnancy belly on, when she looked up and saw Kiana with a shit eatin' grin plastered across her face.

Chapter 9

Daku drove the tan military jeep up the mountainside while Prince Bontana sat in the passenger seat taking in his country's view. He couldn't believe that after all these years he was about to be reunited with the only surviving member of his family.

"I never thanked you for saving my life." Prince Bontana said.

"I never did. Information has prolonged it. Your life may very well be taken if you are lying to me," Daku said, looking over at the Prince. "And if this is a set up, don't think for a second that I won't squeeze the trigger of my AK-47 until there is nothing left of you." Prince Bontana turned away from Daku and began to take in more of the view.

"I know how strong willed you are, Daku. You get it honest. You are your father's son."

His statement was meant to rattle Daku and it worked like a charm. Daku was curious as ever. The Prince knew that the jewel he just dropped on Daku would make him ask question after question, but he wouldn't answer anything until the timing was right, and only then would he open his eyes to the world around him. When Daku asked the first, he only smiled and left him to his thoughts. "You know my father?"

Prince Bontana pointed ahead with his finger. "The village is just around those trees."

They pulled into a remote village and Daku parked the jeep on a dirt patch close to a fenced in garden. Surrounding a lake where the villagers fished were tall leafy banana trees, pear trees, and apple trees with the brightest red and yellow fruit one would ever see in life. Daku was impressed with the small paradise, though his harden expression didn't let on.

There were children at play and women in front of their woven huts washing clothes. When the engine was cut and they stepped out, everyone seemed to simultaneously stop what they were doing. The first person to greet them was someone Daku took to be the village nurse because of her untainted white attire, demeanor, and posture. She held Prince Bontana's hands up to her forehead then kissed each of them.

"Greetings my Prince. You look flushed. Is everything okay with you?" she asked, putting a caring hand to the back of his neck and then to his cheek.

Prince Bontana took her roaming hand into his and patted it. "I'm okay, Samyah. You worry yourself too much," he said with a fatherly smile.

"Anyway Samyah, this here is an old friend." Samyah looked at Daku. Then took a closer look. Tears began to build in her eyes. A single one spilled over, then a few others. The dam had been broken. She slowly released the Prince's hand and put both of hers to her mouth in utter disbelief as she inched closer to Daku. They both seemed to remember each other, him by her name and her by his face.

Daku's mind took a quick trip to the past, placing himself in the same setting with Samyah.

"Is this real?" Daku asked Samyah.

*****

She gave his hand a tempered swat and he released the dried toad back into the bowl of mushroom caps. "My aunt would not like you touching her things, Daku."

He looked around the living room quarter of the well-kept shack at all the artifacts that made a witch's house a home and was dumbstruck.

"My brothers Kenji and Rahmi told me stories of your aunt, the Witch Lady."

"Don't be mean, Daku. My aunt is a doctor, not a witch." she said.

"Well, witch doctor or not, she have things in here to scare kids."

Samyah rolled her eyes at him and said, "Only scary kids."

"I'm not scary. I'm Daku. I'll be a king one day and you'll be my queen."

"Never!"

"Oh yes you will." He stepped closer to her, invading her space. "And would you like to know why?"

"No, I don't need to know," she sassed. "But for the sake of having fun tell me why."

"Well, it's a secret. So if I tell you, I have to whisper it to you in your ear."

Samyah looked around the room and put her hands on her hips. "That's crazy. There's no one here."

"My secret, my rules. So do you want to know or not?"

Samyah huffed. "Fine." She leaned her ear in for him to tell his secret, but Daku had no plans for telling her any secret. He turned her head slightly to face him and planted a quick kiss on her lips. She pulled away instantly.

"Daku, that wasn't nice," she said, wiping her mouth.

"It was for me," he teased.

Samyah had actually liked the kiss Daku stole from her. No boys ever pursued her because they all believed the witch would curse them if they looked in her direction. That may have had something to do with her aunt catching a group of boys laying claim to Samyah and her shaking her beads at them, threatening to curse them if they ever looked her way again.

Daku had heard the tale but refused to entertain such things. He was a brave nine year old with dreams of ruling Africa, and he knew that he could not rule if he had fear. Knowing that, he never ran from a challenge. Samyah was his eleven-year-old lioness and he'd promised to have her when they were adults.

*****

Standing face to face with a different set of circumstances so incomprehensible that they couldn't even begin to put into play the unscripted events that took too many years to unfold. He believed everyone from his village to be dead. Daku's eyes touched Samyah's face like prickly fingertips over brail. His eyes slowly moved over her, taking in every detail of her face as if he were etching it into his memory, each wrinkle of her quivering lips, every fiber of hair. He could not believe he was laying eyes on the prettiest girl he'd ever known all grown up into the woman he never knew existed, until now.

Samyah couldn't resist cupping Daku's face in her hands to look at him. Face full of scars, hardened features, and a rough, patchy beard couldn't overshadow the bright brown eyes of the nine-year-old boy she saw within.

"Daku?" she asked assiduously.

He took her hands in his and brought them to his open nostrils to breathe the quintessence of her life. "It is you," he said. To his amazement, she still looked the same as she did nine years ago. Samyah couldn't stop crying tears of joy as she gazed into Daku's eyes.

"Yes," she answered, her voice trembling. She brought his hands to her nose to smell. "And you are you." She breathed deeply and smiled brightly.

"I've heard stories of you rising through the ranks of the rebels and ... Well, you know. But I didn't believe one word to be true. Not one word of it."

The truth that she'd heard was of Daku leading his Rebel Army on raids and the mass murder of entire cities, even Abdu didn't agree with the ideology of the General. But had Samyah understood politics and strategy, she would've known that Daku was only using the power of his army to eliminate obstacles that would later challenge him when he became a king of a united Africa. Prince Bontana put a hand on Samyah's shoulders.

"Not now young lady." Then to Daku he said, "She's just excited."

"I understand."

"Well, you two must be famished," Samyah considered.

"You sure know what to say to get a man's belly ready for a return feast, don't you, Samyah" Prince Bontana said. "Now let Daku's hands go so that I may show him around. You two can catch up later." He looked at Daku sincerely.

"I believe you will discover that you two will have plenty of time."

Prince Bontana knew that if Samyah stayed any longer she would talk Daku into a coma. That would be too much for a man to handle after such a journey, though he knew Daku wouldn't mind. After all, they had a history no amount of time apart could tarnish.

"She's really very passionate."

"Is this really real?" Daku asked, smelling his hands as he watched Samyah saunter off to a large hut. He could see her smiling from the back. "Is she a nurse of some sort?"

"Yes," the Prince said. "She is a doctor. Home schooled by her aunt who passed away only months ago. The one you as a child believed to be a witch." Daku laughed. "Yes. Children can be very imaginative. Nevertheless, I'm sorry to hear of her passing."

"We'll heal."

"In time," Daku said. The Prince nodded in humble agreement. "And the other reason I'm here ... is it true?"

"Yes, Daku. You will soon see. But first, let me show you around and by the end of your tour everything should be in place. Water?"

"Yes."

"Then let's walk, we'll drink from the spring."

Daku tried to get Prince Bontana to share with him about his father, but all he got was, "In due time it will all come together." But he wanted to know now. He couldn't believe a man from a distant part of the land knew more about his past than he did, and he was the one living his life. How is this possible?

Approaching the village from the trail behind it leading from the forest of old trees, the men could smell all the spices bubbling from the roasting goats and chickens slain for the meal. The ginger and curry injected into the grub worms accented the assemblage of smells emitting from the grills and pots hanging over open fires. Three beautiful young women dressed in flowered gowns and garments wrapped about their heads greeted them when they made it inside the village.

They led the men to Prince Bontana's immaculate hut and there the men had a seat outside on the woven thrones. The women kneeled to undo Daku's boots and slip the Prince's sandals off. A couple of clay pottery bowls of water were brought out with fragrances and petals of different sorts floating atop the water. The men's feet were washed thoroughly then patted dry and new sandals were put on them. Daku felt he could get used to this type of treatment.

"I see you smile outwardly," Prince Bontana taunted.

"No, I..."

"No need, Daku," he said modestly to wane over Daku's embarrassment. "To be honest with you, it's like my first time every time because I appreciate the entire situation and privilege." Daku only nodded. "Ready to eat?"

"Very."

A decorative hand woven carpet as wide as the hut known as The Garden, had been laid out and an assortment of dishes were strewn about in the center. Everything was served on the finest baked clay or huge banana leaves. Dinner placement was broken down into rank. The elders sat around the Prince along with Samyah and Daku, but across from each other in what seemed like a naturally formed circle. The hunters ate amongst themselves, and the women and children formed a group. There was music, singing and dancing as the community broke bread over a feast fit for a king. Samyah couldn't stop smiling over at Daku as she ate modestly from a clay bowl.

Daku returned the gesture. Suddenly the Prince stood, laughing heartily as the guest he had been waiting to return finally walked into the Garden with his wife and two young sons in tow. Daku couldn't believe his eyes. Prince Bontana had been truthful. He sat looking at the only man alive he had a true relation with. He locked eyes with him. He immediately stopped smiling at the Prince's giddy behavior when he saw Daku seated amongst his people staring at him. He approached Daku slowly through the path they made for him. When he got to Daku, he could not stand so Prince Bontana helped him to his feet.

"It's alright brother," he said, holding him up by the shoulders, looking deep into his pained, brown eyes.

"Rahmi?"

"Yes, brother. Who else?" he laughed, then pulled him in and hugged him tight. Daku hugged him back even tighter and made his hands into fists, not wanting to ever let go. A tear escaped his eye.

"I thought you were dead."

*****

The General and Abdu were in the back of his black Lincoln Town Car, having just left the shipyard where the General made adjustments with the men who were putting the finishing touches on his yacht.

"Do you think it was a wise choice to let Daku take the journey alone, General?" Abdu asked with a concerned look on his face.

"Daku is spirited, don't you agree?" the General asked.

"Yes but..."

"Nothing will befall him. Allah's plan is manifesting itself and the time has come for Daku to learn his truth just as it is time for me to let him become the man he is destined to be."

Abdu shook his head. "And where does this leave me when you follow through with this plan of yours?"

"In good hands, my faithful friend."

"How do you plan to get the first piece of business in order?"

"The morning I know he is to return." The General walked over and put his arms around Abdu's shoulder. "We can't fuck this up. I never cut the grass; I'll never see the snakes."

CHAPTER 10

Mika held the Illinois marriage license up to her lips and kissed it. "Thank you! Thank you!"

"You're gonna make some young man very happy," Father Sebastian said ethically.

"If you only knew," she commented snidely.

"Uh-hmm," he cleared his throat with his palm upward and out.

Mika looked at it with disgust and scoffed, "Oh ye of the bullshit clothe."

"Say what you will sister, we all gotta eat."

Mika reached into her purse. "You know what?" She put a couple hundred dollars in his hand. "I ain't even gonna go there. Just have your jiggly throat ass at the jail tomorrow or I'll bleed all the gravy out your slimy ass."

"You can bet your sweet chocolate ass I'll be there. I love it when you talk dirty to me. But if you bent me over and beat me, I'd like that better." He put the hundred dollar bills in his inner breast pocket and pulled out his flask. "Sure you don't just wanna just keep the money?" He held the flask up to Mika then took a swig. She frowned. "Just being sure," he said with a perverted twang. Her phone started ringing. Right on time.

"You'll get the other three hundred after you tie the knot."

"Oh, I can tie it alright."

"Ugh," she hissed, then turned her back to walk away. She put her phone to her ear while at the same time receiving a picture message. "Hello?"

"Bitch, you see my mafuckin' mouf?"

"Who is this?" she asked, knowing damn well who it was.

"Bogus, bitch!"

"I am aren't I?" she replied, ending the call. She looked at the picture message he'd sent her. It was a picture of his mouth and what looked like small cauliflowers covering it. She fell out laughing then forwarded it to Tiara who then put Bogus on blast all over Facebook and Twitter. Mika also forwarded the picture to one of her homegirls in the hood; a thug ass white bitch named Dajuana who she knew would forward the picture around the city.

"You one crazy bitch," Dajuana texted her.

"You ain't kno?" Mika texted back.

*****

Later that night Mika eased toes first into a hot bath laced with peach bath beads, apricot soft soap by Avon, and a light scented bath oil by Oil of Olay. The coconut candle's light danced over everything in her large bathroom. R. Kelly's "Etcetera" off the R. album pumped through her surround sound system to take her mind halfway to the relaxed state she was looking for.

The blunt of Kush she had rolled up on the glass and pearl bath table beside her was gonna do math with the other half. Mika couldn't remember a time she felt so at ease. Maybe the fact that she was about to be filthy ass rich had something to do with it. Still, the battle wasn't over. Soon it would be though.

Jaheim had started to sing "Just In Case" when the water in the tub became noticeably cold, forcing Mika to get out and rinse off in the shower. Once out, she patted herself dry then oiled her body. She stepped out the bathroom into her adjoining bedroom almost losing her footing because Nikki was stretched out on her queen-size bed and silk sheets in nothing but a black-laced thong.

"How in the fuck did you get in?"

Nikki caressed Mika's side of the bed then patted the spot as a gesture for Mika to come have a seat. "You must forget, Mommia, my first hustle was B&E. Now come over here and let me do to you what a man won't do."

Mika smiled and stayed in the bathroom doorway. "First of all, men line up in droves just to eat my shit. So I know they'll do whatever for a bitch. Secondly, I shoulda known something was up when I heard Jaheim come on. I know damn well I ain't have that shit nowhere near my disc changer."

Nikki leaned on her elbow, propping her head in the palm of her hand. She patted the soft spot on Mika's side of the bed again. "Are you gonna come over here or not," she whined.

Mika turned off the bathroom light and proceeded across the room to her nightstand. "I can't. Not tonight anyways."

Nikki sat up. "Why not?" she pouted.

"Because," was all Mika said in response, as she took a seat in front of her vanity. She sprayed on her favorite perfume.

"See, I knew this was gonna happen. That's why I didn't wanna fuck that African booty scratcher ma'fucka."

Mika fell out. "Bitch, you crazy. You know you wanted that dick. The way you sounded when you let me hear you getting yo back beat the fuck out. Please." She turned away from the mirror to face Nikki. "But on the real it ain't even about that."

Nikki had a solemn look on her face. "Well, what else could it be?"

Mika turned back to the vanity. "Girl, boo, miss me with them pouty lips. I just got some other shit on my plate right now, that's all," she said, looking at Nikki through the mirror. "And trust, you don't want no parts of it."

Nikki thought for a second but didn't comprehend any of it so she let it go up and over her head. She got up and put on a flowered silk robe. "Anyways, so tomorrow the big day, huh?"

"Yep,"

"You ready?"

"As ready as a bitch who finna touch all her dreams should be."

"Well don't forget about me."

"You know I won't," Mika sang. "Did you bring the papers for me?"

"Yep." Nikki retrieved the papers and handed them to Mika.

"Here you go."

Mika looked them over. After her personal approval, she said, "Tomorrow after the deal is done, we'll go celebrate."

"Bet that up, Mommia" Nikki replied and they dapped.

The next morning Mika was out the door at eight a.m. to make sure everything was in order by nine. When she meant everything, she meant the preacher's drunk, nasty ass. To her surprise he was sleeping in his beat up 2001 Buick something before she got to the jail. He wasn't about to miss that other three hundred dollars. He needed that to keep Gabby and Tabby around, the meth heads he had lined up to party with all day. She tapped on his driver side glass. He had to stir awake before he realized where he was and the mission at hand.

"You ready?" she asked through the window.

The pink and purplish flab underneath his two chins jiggled when he nodded his head.

"Hell yeah, let's go," he responded quickly and sprinted to the inside where the marriage would take place. After the less than ceremonious ceremony, Father Sebastian took his money and left so fast that his shadow had to catch up. Mika and Shaka were awarded an hour long chaperoned contact visit at ten o'clock in the jailhouse library to kick it after they were married, but Shaka knew Correction Officer Boyte and had less than persuaded him to take the stack Mika had for him to step just outside the door for a few minutes.

"Damn baby, I been waiting on this day for so long," Shaka said, scooping Mika up in his arms and spinning her around.

"Hold on, bae. My stomach."

He put her down. "Oh shit! My bad, boo. You okay?" he asked with concern.

"Yeah, I'm cool," she said, rubbing her tummy.

Shaka put his hand on her stomach. "Does he move, you know, kick and shit like that?"

"Sometimes. Mostly when I eat Mexican food."

"Oh yeah? Let me see your stomach."

She knew Shaka's ass might try to pull that one so she put a full spandex body suit on over her maternity hook-up so that he would not be able to lift it up and discover she was playing him for the dough he didn't know anything about yet. "I can't let you see. I put a spandex body suit on that's suppose to cut down on stretch marks of you stickin' your dick in me and bustin' off."

"Pregnancy is suppose to be natural girl. That's the beauty of it. Stretch marks and all."

She took Shaka's hand and put it between her legs where she'd cut a convenient slit in her pants and body suit to give access to her honeycomb sugar walls. "Shut up, damn. Just feel this pussy on your finger tips for a minute."

Shaka smiled. "I knew you wouldn't let me down."

"For a stack, I bet not," she professed, reaching for his dick meat. He put Mika up on the desk and stood between her legs, dick harder than level ten on Contra. He was ready to put his wood game down when she pulled back abruptly.

"Yo, what the fucks up?" he asked, breathing heavily.

Mika patted his shoulders and pretended to pant or need water or something.

"Heww, hold up, bae. Before I forget," she pulled some papers from her purse along with a pen, "I need you to sign over your power of attorney to me."

Shaka slapped the papers from her hand to the floor. "You mean to tell me you stopped my grove for this bullshit?" They locked eyes. "Man, if you don't lay back and let me hit what's mine."

Mika shoved his ass in the chest. "You better pick them papers up and sign 'em, I ain't for your shit. You know business comes before pleasure." Shaka picked the papers up. Mika held out a pen. "What I need to sign power of attorney bullshit for and I don't have shit to power over?"

"It's so I can set up shit like a college account for your son while your black ass is in here." She pushed the pen at him.

"Now sign the papers while my pussy still wet and wanting that hard dick in me."

Shaka was signing so fast it was scary. When a dick get brick ain't nothing it won't do for relief, she thought.

"That's just like you, always about some business, even after knowing I ain't fucked since God knows when." He threw the papers and pen to the side. "Now don't interrupt me again or I'ma catch a body in this bitch."

Mika grabbed Shaka by the collar and pulled him in.

"Stop bitchin' and fuck me hard, you big dick ma'fucka," she demanded. He obliged.

Shaka took his dick by the base and shoved it in Mika's wet wet. After four hard strokes, he was shaking and shootin' like Ike in Tina when he took her on the counter top.

"Goddamn, I didn't think I was gone do that." Mika laughed. "I know my pussy good, but damn, bae, you breakin' records." Shaka pulled out and put his meat up.

"Ain't shit funny. It's been a minute, shit."

"It's all good. We married now." Shaka rubbed his head in disbelief.

"That's crazy, ain't it?"

"Not to me."

"Why not to you?"

"Because I love you and you love me and we havin' a baby."

"Yeah, that's crazy too."

Visitation only lasted a few more minutes so in that time Shaka did most of the talking while Mika listened to him daydream about coming home soon to her and Shaka Jr.

"So, lil Kiana ain't tried to come up here since that last time has she?"

"You must ain't heard."

"Heard what?" Mika asked, listening intently.

"She was in an accident. Somebody hit her with a car and fled. She's in a coma and shit lookin' real sideways," he said somberly.

"Oh, send her my best."

On Mika's way home she made a special call to Bruce World, the attorney she hired to take Shaka's case. Normally Bruce wouldn't meet a client on his family time, but Mika was everything short of normal so he agreed to meet her at the spot they had met last, Hopper's Secret. It was a car hotel that charged by the hour and kept everything discreet. You pay the gatekeeper, pull into an empty car stall, and handle your business.

Bruce was hoping to get some pussy. Mika wasn't necessarily fond of fucking the dumb dick white boy, but since he felt the need to play her less than the bitch she was, she would send him home with a brand new gift package for his wife. She hadn't even bothered to stop and wash Shaka's nut outta her pussy. She felt Bruce needed to taste another niggaz nut on top of giving him the surprise of his life. And just as legend would have it, a white boy with no dick had a stupid eat 'em up game. And Bruce could eat the bottom out of a pussy majestically. After all of two minutes he came. But Mika told him that if he nutted in her that she would bust a cap in his ass.

"And you bet not get that shit on my clothes or seats!" So when Bruce pulled out, he bust in his hand. "Now eat that shit like a good boy."

When he did, Mika smiled. Nasty ma'fucka.

"Now check this here," she began, "I got these papers," she said going into her purse, "notarized by the county clerk and signed by Bryce. Here," she said, handing him the papers. He immediately took a look at them. His eyes bulged when he peeped the play.

"Does he know what he's done?"

"He will Monday when you sit down and give it to him. Sometime after lunch would be good. And not a minute before." She held up his driver's license. The driver's license that she'd picked him for while he called himself fucking. Then she pocketed it. He knew the play. He'd seen a thousand movies, including *Set It Off* when Queen Latifah did the same shit to the white girl.

"Okay, say I play along with this," he held up the papers, "because these are not the original documents. So I'm assuming you have those, and I don't fuck up what you got going on because you can't capitalize until Monday anyways, are you gonna break me off?"

"That would be your million dollar question, wouldn't it?"

He smiled. "I like how you put that. I won't see him til three in that case."

"Now get the fuck out of my car. I hate snake mufuckas."

*****

Now before I bring Chapter ten to a close, let me give you a quick rewind behind the scene. Right here should be fine.

"I have good news, boo," Nikki said after sucking his dick til his balls had drawn up.

"Great, wat tease it?"

"I've located Shaka's wife," she proudly stated, climbing up to nestle on his chest.

"His wife, huh? 'Ow is dat benaficial to me? I need Shaka."

"Baby, she can take the papers to him and have him sign them. She'll make it so he won't even put up a fight. I always hear you say you hope he doesn't challenge the situation or make this ordeal drawn out. Well, if she went to him, it would make this whole thing that much easier."

Salomon thought about that for a minute. He only had a few days left before Luis and his other partners returned from the West Coast and he wanted this small piece of business handled.

"You are sure dat she con get dem to sign?"

She looked up from his chest and into his eyes. "Boo, is a pig's pussy pork?"

*****

Later that night Nikki broke into Mika's home and attempted to seduce her before handing the contracts over along with the power of attorney papers that she requested.

"Did you bring the papers for me?"

"Yep." Nikki handed her the papers. "Here you go."

"Tomorrow after the deal is done, we'll go celebrate."

97

CHAPTER 11

"The rebels, the ones you control now, raiding our village was nothing short of personal," Rahmi was saying as he and Daku walked a trail through the woods. "Hate killed our family Daku, not war as you may have believed all these years."

Daku recounted what he'd witnessed that happened in the hut the day of the raid and how he had killed the soldier who raped and killed Shassy. "And even after that, I still don't feel like I've gotten any closer to retribution. I aim to kill everyone, tracing back to the ones who killed our family. Rahmi, I have to."

Rahmi stopped abruptly and turned to Daku. "Brother, the raid wasn't about our people, or our family. And the source you seek to kill has already left this Earth."

"But it still happened to our people and our family."

"True, but the rebels had one purpose."

"And what was that?"

"To kill you, brother," Rahmi stated in all seriousness.

"To kill me?" Daku asked, taken aback. "I was nothing more than a child. How could my life be worth enough to award such an atrocity?"

"Because of who you are, Daku. Because of who your father is."

"My father?"

"Yes."

"Why are you the second one to mention something to me about a man I've never met and then refuse to talk to me any further as if it's the secret I'm never supposed to know? Are we keeping secrets, brother?"

Rahmi held Daku's arm. "*Never!* Walk with me and I'll brief you on who you are, and then you'll understand." They continued up the trail in silence until they came upon a cliff and stood next to a waterfall.

"A long time ago your father had fallen in love with a woman, but they could never be together. Nonetheless, they couldn't stay away from each other. Your father's father, Las Surh, was the King of Tanzania and his adversary, Ansuul Leer, was the King of Angola, but they both had an enemy more powerful than them both; the King of Egypt, Asu Rah. He could call upon the armies of Algeria, Libya, Chad, and Sudan because he had conquered their lands and in order for their kings to stay in power, they had to agree to fight with Asu anytime he called upon them.

With such power, Asu then wanted to bully Ethiopia, but when your grandfather got wind of this, he united his Tanzanian army then summoned Ansuul Leer, the King of Angola, to fight with them because it was apparent to Las Surh, your grandfather, that Asu Rah would not stop until he conquered all of Africa.

"Your grandfather knew that together they could overthrow Asu Rah. He knew that if they put their differences aside that every nation from the Congo down to South Africa would aid in their fight. In order for the united front to truly be united, your grandfather gave your father away to wed Zakyra, the King of Angola's daughter. Shortly after the union of the nations, Zakyra became pregnant with a daughter she named Danora. As planned, your grandfather's side won the war. Asu Rah was forced back to Egypt to lick his wounds. But their glorious celebration was short lived, with your father and his wife that is."

"Why?"

"Because your father could never love his wife the way he did your mother, Daku."

The gravity of what was being said weighed on Daku as he took it all in and began to sort it all out. Then Rahmi continued. "When Zakyra found out about your father sneaking into another woman's home to consort with her, she went into a rage. She was the one who took a part of your father's personal army and formed the rebels you rule today. Their mission was to find your mother and kill her. But when they found her, she was pregnant, which made the rebels question their position. Had your father known this secret sect had been formed, he would have killed the men involved because he loved your mother with all of who he was." Both men took a long breath.

"Anyways, they took your mother back to Zakyra to a place outside the city where she was held up in secret and there, Zakyra beat your mother into labor. Once she had given birth to you, your father's wife gave you to the rebels, who in turn took you to the trash heap where Shassy found you. It's believed Zakyra couldn't bring herself to kill you and your mother so she exiled your mother instead of spilling her blood. She did all of this behind your father's back. Your mother believes your father looked for both of you day and night and never stopped."

Daku could not believe what he was hearing. "All of this time," he said with his head held low. "He knew. He knows. How could I have missed it?"

"You couldn't have known, Daku," Rahmi assured him. "But soon you will know everything."

"If all you say is true, and the General is my father, then who is my mother?" Rahmi pointed down to the riverbank at a woman washing clothes by hand in the river.

"She is there, Daku."

CHAPTER 12

"Mommia, you mean to tell me I that got all jazzed up in this fya ass gear just to sit outside a damn wanna-be studio smokin' blunts? I thought we was gone celebrate?"

"We are gonna celebrate, but later. The first order of business is to eliminate all the thorns in my bush. After that, I can set out to do what I'd planned to do a long time ago."

Nikki inhaled the Kush smoke. "And what's that?"

"Build me an immovable team and run this city."

The street was desolate. Mika sat parked under a busted street light with Nikki posted shotgun, clueless as to why she was really there. At the end of the block was a fenced-in building used as a studio by a crew from the Flux known as The Currency Exchange Gangstas. They made a name for themselves by robbing, killing, selling dope, and selling underground mixtapes that told horrific stories about the shit they did in real life. Mika reached in the back seat of the black Camry she bought from a hype over a week ago. She had formulated a plan. Pulling a briefcase onto her lap, she popped the latches and flipped the lid open revealed the Tec-9mm inside.

Nikki's eyes bucked and she choked on the Kush smoke. "What the fuck?"

Mika screwed the cooler onto the gun and put the clip in...*Klack Klack.*

"The back light in the building just went out," Mika said. "Take my seat and keep the lights out. When I finish dumpin', pull up to pick up."

"What the fuck, Mommia?"

Mika was out the car tip toeing up the block like a black panther, clinging to the shadows with the adept stealth of a Navy Seal operative, Tec-9 at her side.

*****

"Yo my nigga, that verse you spit was some Biggie type shit," Loonie Tunes said to Legend through the mic from the controls so that he could hear him inside the booth. "Now do your ad libs and we can wrap this session up. I'll mix the shit down at the crib."

"Bet," Legend said into the mic. "It's a mothafucka up in here."

"We almost done now my nigga. From the top." Legend adjusted his headphones and wiped sweat from his brow. "I'm ready."

Loonie Tunes hit the space bar on his computer and the beat played from the top. "Pass the blunt Pony Boy," Loonie Tunes said to Pony Boy, who sat on the leather couch behind him with Rah Rah, smoking all the weed.

"Man, you better hit this shit, Rah. You know when that nigga hit the shit it's gonna come back wet," Pony Boy said to Rah Rah. "Nigga, fuck you. I don't never be wettin' that shit. It be wet when you lil niggaz pass it is what it is."

"Yeah right," Pony Boy whispered, passing Rah Rah the blunt.

"Man, you better hit it first."

"That's it fool," Loonie Tunes said with the blunt hanging from his thick lips, shutting down the equipment as Legend left out the booth, hanging the headphones on the mic.

"Man," Legend breathed.

"I'm ready to get up out this bitch. What time we gone meet up at the club?"

"I know I need bout an hour or so to change and it's whatever after that," Pony Boy said.

"Sounds good to me," Rah Rah added.

"Aiight, since all that bullshit squared, you niggaz can go out the front door and I'll make sure the back locked down tighter than boy pussy in a D.C. jail," Loonie Tunes joked.

"Man, you bogus. I'm from D.C. ma'fucka," Rah Rah said.

"Even worse," Loonie Tunes countered.

"Fuck you in yo pussy nigga," Rah laughed. "I'll help you lock down in the back."

"Nah, I got it. Just make sure y'all drop the steel latch and lock the bottom on y'all way out."

"Aiight fool. We gone meet you around the side," Legend said.

"Aiight. I'ma kill these lights and lock up. Have a blunt waitin' on me."

"Hell nah, wet mouf ass mufucka. You just fucked up the last cypher with the blunt," Rah Rah shot back causing everyone to erupt in laughter.

Loonie Tunes felt some kinda way about the joke but brushed it off. "Ha ha, punk ass. Just lock the door and have that shit ready." He went to the back of the studio and hit the lights before locking the back door. Legend was the last one out the front door and he made sure the bottom lock was on before he shut it and pushed the steel latch so that the plate would draw behind the door to secure it.

"Oh shit!" Rah Rah said, reaching for his waist.

Legend tried to fall back inside the front door but had locked himself out only seconds before.

Mika came from around the corner of the studio and opened fire on the three men. Rah Rah was the first to fall, succumbing to a fatal headshot that took a quarter chunk of his cranium.

Pony Boy caught a shoulder shot and bitched up. "Please don't! *Lord No!* Please don't kill me!"

As Mika riddled him with bullets, Pony Boy's body slumped forward and blood began to spread like a small crimson pond around his lifeless body.

Legend got off a shot and hit Mika square in the chest with his .380. She fell back. "Stupid bitch! You thought it was that easy," he barked, standing over her. Loonie Tunes came from around the corner, gun drawn.

"What the fuck, Slow?" he asked Legend, aka Slow.

"This bitch tried to catch me slippin', G."

"Oh yea?" he said, blowing Slow's face to the other side of the street. He then helped Mika to her feet by extending a hand to her.

"You good, ma?"

She lifted her shirt and unsnapped her vest to relieve the burning. She took a moment to catch her breath, the bullet had knocked the wind out of her. "Yeah, I'm good."

"Cool, your ride here. I'll meet you at the club. Gimme an hour or so to handle this shit."

"Aiight," she said, running to the car inconspicuously ducked low.

*****

2 Chainz was pumping and the club was packed from wall to wall, every baller and sack chaser was in attendance. Gold and diamonds glistened and glittered everywhere under the

colorful strobe lights. "Man that shit wild, ma. You fuckin' crazy," Loonie Tunes said to Mika as they sat drinking Patron in the VIP section in Club Six Pistols where the noise was minimal.

"Hell yeah she is," Nikki added. "Next time give a bitch the heads up."

"Aiight, aiight, aiight. Enough of that shit," Mika said, trying to hold her own excitement in when she saw the thick ass white girl and bearded brother with the eye patch walk into the club. "Dajuana and Yuseff just came through the door." Mika waved them over once they spotted her behind the glassed-in balcony.

"What up Tunes, Nikki?" Dajuana greeted when she came into VIP.

"What it do my main mafuckin' bitch?" she greeted Mika excitedly.

"What up?" Mika said, giving Dajuana a pound then slapped five three times before they hugged.

"What, you bitches used to play high school ball or some shit?" Loonie Tunes teased about their secret handshake type thingamajig.

Yuseff was a different story when he greeted the crew. "Peace God," he said to Tunes.

"Peace my nigga," Loonie Tunes replied, lifting his glass.

"Peace Earth," he greeted Nikki.

"How you doing, Yuseff?" she said respectfully.

"I'm good," he answered before getting to Mika. "What's the science Queen of the Universe?"

"Math," Mika said.

"My favorite build."

Mika smiled. "That's why we're all here." She loved Yuseff like a brother. He'd just gotten out the joint and was too deep into his Five Percent thing, but she knew the killer and hustler in him still lurked and so did he if she needed him the way she did now.

Mika looked around the room at the four people she had called to this meeting and asked everyone to have a seat.

"We all know each other here, and I know this gathering is to celebrate the beginning of us making a united front to take this city, but first things first. We need to get this business out the way in order to understand what our goal is when we move forward from tonight as a single, well oiled machine."

"That's what's up. Speak on that shit," Loonie Tunes said with his glass raised before taking a sip. "First of all, each one of you have proven your loyalty to me in one form or another, which explains why you sit here now." Each of the participants of the meeting looked at each other and nodded, knowing that Mika's approval made each of them all good.

"The number one thing we are not gonna do is let this money come between us like them punk ass organizations you see in the F.E.D. magazines and shit. There will not be a weak link in this chain. And yes, I know everyone has said that before and shit still gets fucked up somewhere, but that's because somewhere the master link tried to run the empire with some form of fear. I want to show my team love and have y'all love me back. Respect and loyalty is all I ask of you."

Mika looked around the room. "We're about to touch some serious money y'all. More money than we can spend. Dajuana," Mika singled her out.

"What's up?"

"Reach into your pockets and pull out every dollar you have."

All four people in VIP, including Mika, watched Dajuana go through her pockets.

"Here," she said to Mika, holding out the bands of money.

"Loonie Tunes."

"What it do, ma?"

"Take that money from Dajuana."

Loonie Tunes came over and did as she requested.

"Now the rest of you empty your pockets, including you Loonie Tunes, and put that shit in that trash bag on the side of that chair," she said, pointing at the black trash bag she conveniently had stashed there.

Everybody looked at each other amused, wondering what the hell the lesson was in all of the theatrical shit. "I'm glad to see ain't none of y'all trippin'," she smiled.

"Nikki," she said.

"Yeah, Mommia."

"Hand me my hand bag, please."

Nikki reached behind the red leather couch and came up with a black Gucci handbag.

"Here you go. It's kinda heavy."

Mika smiled. "I know. Thank you."

"You're welcome."

She reached in the bag and pulled out fresh bank wrapped ten thousand dollar bundles and handed each person in the room two of them. Each person looked pleased. "We ain't fuckin' with old money no more. Everything we finna touch gone be brand new. Twenty thousand in each of our pockets makes us all equal in this room, but remember, I'm the master link. From me my love will spread to each one of you and with respect and loyalty your love for me will cycle back through each of you. I'll call the shots. Don't no ma'fucka make a move without my say so." She looked around the room, making eye contact.

"We got that part? We all clear?" Everyone nodded. "Good, now down to business." Once Mika laid her game plan out and saw that everyone was eager to play their role, it was time to party.

Everyone in the crew, with the exception of Yuseff, were tipsy when they made their way through the crowd to exit the club which is why he carried the trash bag full of old money with him at his side behind his crew to make sure he could watch their backs in case shit popped off.

All of a sudden, a young dude by the name of Crucial grabbed his wrist, stopping his stride. Crucial said, "What's in the bag homie?" He knew the answer because he could see the shapes the money's impressions made in the bag. Plus Crucial wasn't no little nigga, which is why Yuseff's six four, two hundred seventy pounds didn't intimidate him. He was just as big, if not bigger, black as a midnight shit with a wrinkled baldhead, looking like D-Bo's lil big brother.

Yuseff didn't hesitate. Years of mixed martial arts training from a Brazilian jiu-jitsu street fighter who caught a murder beef while drunk fighting in a bar and ended up being his cellie was about to get put to use. He dropped the bag of money and reversed the grip Crucial had on him, putting so much pressure on his thumb and wrist that he had to drop to one knee. He couldn't believe it... his face twisted as he winced and grimaced in pain. Yuseff quickly let his wrist go and took him by the head, forcing knee after knee into his face. But Crucial fought back, face bloody as hell. He grabbed Yuseff by the legs and took him down. Yuseff, thinking fast, took Crucial by the arm and rolled over with his limb trapped underneath him. All anyone heard was a loud crack that seemed to drown out the music. Crucial hollered so loud it was piercing.

Yuseff rolled over and got to his feet and took a stance that made ma'fuckas back up. Nobody wanted any, especially after seeing Crucial's arm. His shit looked like the only thing keeping it attached to his body was the long sleeve shirt.

"We done here?" Yuseff asked.

Crucial put a hand on his broken arm to hold it close to his body and nodded his head weakly. Yuseff picked up the bag of money. Coming through the crowd was Dajuana with her 9mm drawn.

"Move! Move! Back the fuck up!" When she got to him, she asked, "You okay?"

"I'm good, baby," he answered her.

Mika, Loonie Tunes, and Nikki made it to them when all the commotion allowed them passage.

"Y'all good?" Loonie Tunes asked.

"Yeah, he good," Dajuana spoke up.

"I know he is," Mika said playfully. "Yo ass got back here so fast it was scary," she said to Dajuana.

"Now I see why it's so easy for niggaz to stop eatin' pork but impossible to leave you white bitches alone. You hoes go all out for a black dick." Everyone laughed.

"Fuck you, bitch," Dajuana said with a smile.

"Let's bounce," Yuseff said.

At the club's entrance Mika was bumped into by a stocky built African man with cuts in his face and a scowl to match. He looked at her with so much malice that it shook her more than she would ever admit. To break the eye contact, she looked back to see if her team noticed him as well. They hadn't and within the blink of an eye, he was gone.

What the fuck … impossible, she thought. "I'm trippin'," she mumbled. *Gotta be the liquor*, she thought trying to trick herself into not believing what she saw, but she knew what she saw was real. *Hell naw, I'm trippin. I gotta stop drinkin' fa'real.*

CHAPTER 13

"Hey yo, Vaughn," Shaka heard over the dayroom loudspeaker. "Get your jumpsuit on. You got a visit."

He went to his cell to get dressed and stood at the block door waiting on central to pop the lock so that he could go to the inmate-attorney visiting tank. It was nothing more than a small brick room with a table bolted to the floor and a few fold out chairs.

Bruce World was already in the room dressed casually waiting on Shaka. When he entered the room they shook hands. "Have a seat," Bruce said. Shaka sat across from him.

"What's up? I hope you got some good news about my case," Shaka said with a trace of excitement.

Bruce wove his fingers together and leaned forward on the table. "Actually, this visit has nothing to do with your case, although I have good news for you pertaining to your situation nonetheless."

"So if you ain't come to talk about my case, what did you come for?"

"Let's go with the bad news first," Bruce said, retrieving his briefcase, snapping the latches as he sat it on the table.

"Bad news?"

"Yes," he answered, handing him the papers from the briefcase. Shaka took them and glanced at the first sheet. "Do you recognize the papers you're looking at?"

Shaka saw that it was the power of attorney papers Mika had brought for him to sign. He tossed them on the table.

"Yeah I seen 'em, so what?"

"So what do you think of it all?"

"I don't think shit. My wife brought the papers here for me to sign so that she can handle our affairs while I'm in here."

Bruce picked up the papers from the table. "Oh I see. If I had a wife I loved, I guess I would trust her with a hundred fifty million dollars of my money too."

"Fuck you talkin' 'bout, nigga?" Shaka asked with surprise. "What hundred fifty million you know about that I don't?" He snatched the papers back, slowly flipping through them, finally reading them thoroughly.

Once he was done he asked, "How is this shit real? I don't have no family with no diamond mines, especially not in Africa. I'm from Miami."

"Well, apparently you do. Your real father located you somehow before his passing away and sent some of his company partners over here so that you could get what was rightfully yours. Instead, your wife," he said with quotation fingers, "settled your affairs with a business buyout using that contract you hold in your hands signed by you."

"I don't understand."

"Why didn't you read the documents before you signed them?" Bruce asked, playing dumb.

Shaka thought back to being caught in the moment standing between Mika's legs, dick harder than a mothafucka, needing to get that nut. Then he thought about something. "Wait, how did you get the papers?" Caught off guard, Bruce stumbled with his words.

"How long you had 'em? It's damn near five o'clock in the evening and you just now coming to see me?"

Bruce started to pack up his shit so that he could get the hell outta dodge. He could feel the heat emitting off of Shaka. "My paralegal had the documents to look through them to make sure they were indeed legit before I brought them to your attention."

"How long you been in cahoots with that bitch?"

"Wa. . .What?"

"Don't play me Bruce, or I'll beat you unconscious where you stand. *HOW LONG!*" He hissed.

"She came on to me, I swear," Bruce pleaded. "Please don't do anything you're gonna regret later," he said in almost a whimper as Shaka was making his way around the table.

"What's your cut? How much that bitch pay you to throw that shit in my face? Because fa'real fa'real, she didn't need you once I signed the papers."

"I don't know what you're talking about when you ask that."

Shaka was around the table with one hand on the back of Bruce's neck and the other on his arm. "What's the good news? Didn't you say there was good news?"

"Yeah. There's good news."

"So spit it out."

"I worked out a deal where you only have to serve six months county time if you don't go to trial. The state only wants a conviction. They know you didn't fire your gun that night because ballistics show that your gun was never fired, plus they never swabbed your hands for residue, which would've proven it."

"Well, why not just get me off?"

"Because they'll drag me for a year and you'll have done the six months anyways."

Shaka thought about the deal for a minute. "Make it happen. Bitch can't spend that much money by then." Shaka shook Bruce hard. "And if I were you, when I come home I wouldn't be able to be found."

"Alright, alright. I swear I'll be gone. You have my word."

"But in the meantime," he straightened Bruce's clothes, fixing his shirt collar, "I'd make sure that my beautiful wife didn't find out when I'm coming home."

"Okay, you have my word."

"Good."

CHAPTER 14

"The wire transfer was successful, baby girl," Mika said to Nikki over the phone. "We're paid bitch. Tell your boy it was nice doing business with him."

The early morning sun was baking Nikki's beautiful skin as she sat on the twenty-sixth floor patio of the Claymore Hotel in a platinum colored silk robe that hung open to reveal her sky blue laced panty and bra set while eating fresh mango and strawberries, getting her feet massaged by Salomon. "Boo, Shaka's wife said thank you for your business."

He kissed her big toe. "Tell her she's welcomb."

"He says you're welcome. Anyways, when we suppose to hook up? We need to talk."

"I don't know, me and Loonie Tunes headed up north to check out the mansions that way."

Nikki pouted. "That's no fair. I should be a part of that Mommia."

"Bitch, you don't know shit about securing no shit like that so quit. Plus, it'll be a surprise what I decide on, and you'll be able to help decorate. Some shit these niggas don't know shit about."

Nikki smiled bright. "When you put it that way, I can't wait."

"I know, boo boo. Chow," Mika said, ending the call.

When she and Loonie Tunes made it out to Shannandova, the mansion district where only the elite lived on nothing less than twenty acres, they met with a broker named Mary Garrison who was a gorgeous redheaded white woman about twenty-six or so, dressed in an all red Versace body skirt that clung to her curves. Her white Jimmy Choo three-inch heel sandals were on point too. Mika gave her a woman's nod of approval because she fucked with the bitch's style. Mary extended her freshly manicured hand.

"Hi, my name is Mary Garrison, the one you spoke with on the phone. How are you? How was your trip?"

"Fine. With so much excitement how could it be anything less?" Mika returned with the same tone as Mary.

Mary extended her hand to Loonie Tunes, who was decked out in an all white Michael Jordan nylon sweat suit with matching 96 Classic shoes and a fat dookie rope with a musical note medallion. His green eyes dazzled in the sun and instantly Mary's pussy soaked her flesh colored thong.

"And you are?"

"I'm yours, but my friends call me Loonie Tunes," he said with the air of a ma'fucka attempting to do spoken word.

Mary smiled bright and her cheeks became flush red. "That's cute."

Mika shook her head. That's the best line this musical ma'fucka got? Who in the fuck would go for that shit but this country ass girl?

Mary turned her attention back to Mika, who had to wipe the silly expression off her face as she watched these two carry on. "I hope you guys are ready to look at some mansions."

"Sure we are," Mika said.

"Great. Lets make a day of it,' Mary said giddily. She turned to walk to the first property they were to look at with a lil more pop in her hips to make Loonie Tunes watch her shapely ass sway. He walked behind her, rubbing his hands together and licking his lips, as if he were about to eat Thanksgiving early this year.

Mika laughed and punched him in the shoulder.

"Let's go freak."

After checking out four huge mansions, Mika fell in love with the one they were coming upon a quarter of a mile up a slight hill hidden behind a fortress of trees surrounding the compound. The mansion was a bone white colonial style with six cathedral type pillars holding up a luxurious balcony that went from each end of the front of the huge historical site. A gate surrounded the top of this mansion.

"Is there a pool up top?" Mika asked excitedly as she gazed up the mansion like it would the Empire State Building.

"Yes, as a matter of fact there's a two hundred square foot pool up there along with a huge Jacuzzi, barbecue pit and full bar. The last owners used to cover the pool with a thick glass and convert the pool into a dance floor when they had gatherings. There's also a basketball hoop so you can play while in the pool."

"Who were the last owners?" Mika asked modestly.

"Barack and Michelle Obama."

"Bullshit!"

"No seriously. Lets get a closer look," Mary invited as she and Mika went on a tour. Loonie Tunes stayed outside to assess the grounds to get a feel for how he would set up security. There was no doubt Mika was about to purchase the mansion.

CHAPTER 15

Daku had never felt so humble and confused in his life. What was he to say to his newly discovered mother? Hello Mother, I'm your long lost son. The one the rebels threw into the trash. No amount of mix-matched words could express the fear clawing at his gut, threatening to come through his stomach and throat. What if this woman rejected him? What then? Would he kill Bontana and everything in his life for trapping him in the worst hoax ever played on a man? Would he kill Rahmi for his disloyalty? And what of Samyah? He still loved her through and through. No amount of time could pass when his love for her would not be. Even in death she was loved.

He had so many questions yet only one important one. *Who am I?*

The woman at the river was bent at the waist wringing a checkered cloth out into the river. She shook it in the air then tossed it into her basket when she noticed Rahmi approaching with a stranger with a familiar face. She tilted her head and her eyebrows furrowed as she took in the features of the man in Rahmi's company. She couldn't believe it. Tears filled her eyes and her hands shot up to cover her mouth as she trembled. Her mind told her to run to the man coming her way and to throw her arms around him, but her legs did not respond.

Daku looked at the woman who Rahmi claimed was his mother, searching for any features they may have shared and never looked further than her eyes. His and hers were one and the same, deep, brown, and pained.

"She remembers you, Daku," Rahmi said to Daku who had his blinders on blocking everything out around him and didn't hear him. Rahmi looked back and forth between the two and figured he wasn't needed for introduction.

"Looks like you two have it. I'll leave you to it," he said. Daku still looked ghost.

"Hello, Kaleah, I'm leaving him with you, will that be okay?" he asked respectfully.

"Yes Rahmi, that is fine." And with that Rahmi turned on his heels and left, smiling inwardly.

"I have prayed every night for many years that you would return to me," Kaleah said in her native tongue. She could not stop the floodgates that her tears continued to escape through.

She fell to her knees on the riverbank rocks with her hands together, thanking God over and over. Daku came over and fell to the ground with her. He put his arms around Kaleah and squeezed her. He could feel the love of all the years she yearned for him pass through their embrace and into his bones. He rocked her back and forth. This was the beginning of his cleansing.

She put her head on his shoulder and squeezed back, smelling him. He smelled so manly. She didn't want to let him go. Her baby had come back to her. A man no doubt, but still her baby regardless. Daku was the first to pull away.

"It's okay, mother. I know what you've had to go through, but I promise, no more, I'm here now."

Kaleah wiped at her eyes. "I can't stop crying," she said with a smile. She fanned her face with her hands.

Daku helped her clear her tears with his thumbs. "I take it you know who I am, yes?"

Kaleah looked him in the eyes as only a loving mother could.

She looked into his eyes as if only one day of absence stood between them and said, "Well, yes." Then she had a thought a Nano second later. "And I heard stories about you," she said, jabbing him in the arm with her sharp knuckled fist playfully.

"How long have you known that I was with the General, my father?" he asked.

The question felt alien on his lips. "And why am I only meeting you now? What is this?"

They sat on the rocks and talked well into the night. Kaleah explained how the General got word to kill Zakyra's nephew. She told him that the General knew immediately who he was.

"So you heard about that?" Daku asked.

"Yes, along with other things."

She told him about the love she and his father shared. Zakyra hated her for having his heart and exiled her for it. She explained how she had no choice but to give him to the rebels that night. "It was a fight I could not win. I was weak."

"It's okay, I'm here."

"Do you wanna know what I named you?" she asked as they approached the village bonfire arm in arm.

"Yes."

People were dancing around a huge fire as the drums and clapping made a beat to groove to. Shit was real live. Everyone was happy. These were good times.

"I named you Jazereek."

Daku looked off into the distance. He liked the name, but he was Daku and it would forever stay that, Granny Tutu would continue to get that much respect, real mama or not.

"Zakyra only died last year. She was the only thing stopping me all these years," Kaleah said sincerely, looking into his bottomless eyes.

"I heard how she died, Daku."

He did not fidget. "Everyone has their secrets, mother. I shall continue to have mine."

Kaleah breathed hard. She too knew all too well how heavy the burdens of carrying secrets could be. "I see a certain someone has had her eye on you since your return."

126

She looked at Samyah, who couldn't stop smiling as she danced the two-step waiting for Daku to come over.

"We have forever Daku. Go get your queen. We can talk tomorrow. You need your rest. There is much more I have to tell you, but don't let that trouble your night. You've waited this long and now the time has come, but for now, enjoy yourself. You two are the spitting image of how me and your father loved."

"Thank you, mother."

"Goodnight son," Kaleah said, patting his arm before retreating to her hut.

Samyah and Daku sat side by side on woven baskets enjoying conversation and laughing at Bontana as he danced some crazy shit with the witch doctor who had a white skull painted on his face, big baboon furs on his shoulders and ankles and big noise-making beads around his neck and wrists.

"The Gods should bless him with some teeth," Daku joked.

"You're not right, Daku," Samyah laughed. Then she looked at him genuinely in the eyes. "I like that you've always been able to be yourself with me."

"That will always be," he responded.

They sat for hours enjoying the festivities. Rahmi had turned in for the night with his family before the night even began, but promised to be up early to catch up more with Daku. Bontana was stoned with the witch doctor and the only thing left for Samyah and Daku to do was go to her hut where he could sleep for the night. Or attempt to....

Kaleah tapped on the entrance of Samyah's hut in the dark of the night when no other citizen of the community was awake. Samyah pulled the curtain back as if she had been expecting her. Daku was sitting in a chair drinking some type of tea and smiled when he saw Kaleah walk in.

"Is there something wrong, mother?"

Kaleah rushed to his side and kneeled to his thigh. "The messenger who brings me word from your father has just left from me with disturbing news," she said urgently with tears in her eyes.

Daku sat his cup on the floor by his foot. "What is it?"

Kaleah became choked up before speaking again. "Your father ... the General is dead."

Daku stood. He lifted his mother by the shoulders. "What? How?"

"The messenger says heart attack." Samyah's hands covered her mouth.

"Heart attack?"

"Yes. I know you want to leave immediately."

"I must," Daku said, turning on his heels headed for the door. "I'll come with you," Samyah said.

"Me too," added his mother,

Daku stopped dead in his tracks and without turning around said, "No, I must go alone. If all is bad when I arrive then I'll send for you." With that he headed for the Jeep. Unbeknown to him Rahmi would be there waiting for him, legs crossed, resting his ass on the hood when he got there.

"News must travel fast in this village," Daku said.

Rahmi uncrossed his legs at the ankles.

"I'm going with you."

"Get the gas cans from the lock box in the back so we can refuel now before we get on the road." Rahmi had a comeback ready on his tongue because he knew his brother would protest. It shocked him that the confrontation he was expecting didn't happen. He got the gas cans and began to refuel.

"Daku," Kaleah called to him. He turned to her. "Come, I have to tell you something very important before you leave. This may be the most important thing you'll ever hear in life and you need to know now."

*****

"And who authorized such a decision?" Daku asked Abdu as he stood over the General's lifeless body. Rahmi was just outside the room.

"The General before his untimely death," Abdu responded.

"Why would the General keep so many secrets? Why would he confide in money hungry board members of his diamond mine business that I never knew he had fifty-one percent control over until now? Why after all these years did he not tell me his history?" Daku asked more to himself than to Abdu.

"Daku, the General was wiser than you think. He said to me that you can't see the snakes if you don't cut the grass. I'm sure that'll mean something to you soon."

Daku thought for a minute. The wrinkles in his forehead and his squinting eyes showed his deep concentration. "Do they know that I'm his son as well?"

"No, they believe that your twin brother, Shaka, is the surviving baby that was tossed into the trash heap. They know nothing of there being two of you."

"How long have Salomon and Luis been gone?"

"Since this morning."

CHAPTER 16

"This building is perfect," Mika exclaimed, clasping her hands in front of her chest.

"Mika, it's a fuckin' outdated school where fucked up kids came to get their GED," Dajuana said distastefully. None of Mika's team shared her enthusiasm.

Mary was excited though. "So I take it you want a tour."

"Hell yeah!" Mika said eagerly.

"I don't know how you pulled this shit off so quick." Loonie Tunes hit Mary's left ass cheek and she jumped.

"Where there's a will there's a way," she giggled.

The building they entered looked like an old firehouse from the outside. The two huge doors that opened French style on the front of the building were so massive that they looked as if one had to have their good deeds outweigh their bad to get in. The inside smelled like old attic books, catching everyone's breath, but the black and white tiled floors were in excellent condition, as were the walls and high ceilings.

Mika couldn't contain how ecstatic she was. Mary knew she would buy it. She'd witnessed the same wild look in Mika's eyes when she purchased the mansion.

Mika led the way through the building as though she knew her way around already. As quiet as it was kept she did because she too had gotten her GED at the school when she was sixteen, thinking she knew all there was to know about life after she had gotten pregnant at fifteen.

*****

"You're not having this baby, bitch!" Charles hissed vehemently at Mika, who sat on the passenger side of his candy apple red Fleetwood Cadillac. Mika was pouting as he drove along aimlessly, wishing he loved her like he said he would when he first stuck his thick crooked thing in her virgin walls. When Mika didn't answer, he reached over and choked her so hard he left his fingerprints in her dark skin. Biting down on his bottom lip and frowning, he said, "You think I'm fuckin' playin' with you?"

Mika's fear poured out through her eyes that were the size of golf balls. She scratched at Charles' hand and forearm. "I can't breave..."

Charles shook her by the neck then forced her head into the window. "Bitch!"

Bi-polar wasn't a hood diagnosis for niggaz around the way. Ma'fuckas was crazy, period...point...blank. And Charles was one crazy nigga. He pulled over on the side street he was coasting and parked behind a Wonder Bread truck. "Look, I'm sorry okay," he said softly to Mika, who was crying hard but struggling to keep her composure.

"Come here," he said, opening his arms. "Come here, baby. I'm so sorry. I never shoulda put my hands on you." He pulled Mika into his embrace. He patted her head on his chest as she labored across the armrest to reach him. "I'm so sorry, I promise. I'm just scared what yo mama would say and do to both us if she knew I was fuckin' her daughter too, ya feel me?"

Mika nodded her head.

"So, you can't be having no baby by me." He reached in his Hugo Boss slacks and peeled five one hundred dollar bills off his knot. "Take this and tomorrow after school I want you to go to the clinic and get that baby outta you. If you don't, I'ma beat it out you, aiight?"

Mika didn't go have an abortion and she couldn't tell her mama that Charles had tricked her into fucking him, her man, and she was having his baby. But when the baby boy was born, it looked like Charles had nutted in his hand, put the shit in his mouth, and spit the baby in Mika.

Cheryl, being hip, saw the baby and knew Charles' no-good ass had been fucking her daughter. But since he paid all the bills and kept her right, she was willing to turn a blind eye to the bullshit if she didn't have to look at the disrespectful baby. They found a family who was willing to buy the baby. Mika was heartbroken, but what could she do?

The fifteen thousand they collected from the family who brought the baby went to Charles to help him advance in the dope game. With that came the big head and Charles traded Cheryl in for a seventeen year old on the west side. Mika's mom blamed her for the loss and looked upon her with great disdain.

A month later Mika was roaming the streets looking for a place to sleep at night. Naïve, Mika got with a pimp named Nickel until he fell victim to one of Shaka's come ups. Shaka found a soft spot for her in his heart so Mika agreed to help him get Nickel's no-good ass.

"That's what you get bitch! My ass says exit only, you sick ma'fucka!" Mika kicked him in the gut with her pointy-toed heels. Seizing the opportunity to get away but was afraid if she let Nickel live he would surely come after them and lock them in the basement and starve them to death like he did Kitty for choosing Briscoe that one time. The smell left behind after Kitty's death was still in her nostrils. With fear in her spirit, she took her box cutter and cut Nickel's throat. Nickel probably choked himself to death trying to stop the bleeding. She didn't stick around long enough to find out.

Mika opened the doors to the cafeteria and was pleased to see there were tables systematically placed for seating and all the stainless steel appliances needed was a good wiping down.

It all looked the same as when she attended the place.

"This is perfect," she beamed.

"Man, fuck you. And if you keep talkin', your job gone be in this kitchen." Yuseff laughed and caught an elbow to the ribs from Dajuana.

"Okay, next," Mika said, wanting to go through the rest of the building.

Fall was biting summer in the ass. The once green leaves on the trees were starting to change to orange and brown. Mika had decorated the mansion and locked it down with heavy security. She turned the building into a type of Black Wall Street, where dope boys could buy bogus stock in exotic pills and office supplies that did not exist to wash their money at a rate of twenty percent with real time paperwork that screamed they were legit. Dope boys from all over the great old U.S. of A. could wash their money with a phone call to any of the twenty operators and the purchase of a stock number. Mika would get her twenty percent cut off the top, pay the IRS their taxes and then send the dealers their money back clean. She'd just legalized selling dope when she made the dope boys pay taxes on the money they collected from their street sales.

"That's all the big fuss is about anyways," Yuseff said, seated across from Mika in her office, which was the classroom she used to take all her tests in.

"Yuseff," she began in a no nonsense tone, leaning towards him behind her red oak desk. She weaved her fingers together. "Let me ask you something."

"There ain't nobody here but me and you, sis. What's up?"

Mika took a deep breath. "What if I told you that I'm pregnant?"

"What?"

"Yep." Mika snickered. "Two months. Karma done come back to bite me in the ass."

"That what's up," he congratulated her until he looked into her face. He sat back in his chair and let out a long breath.

"Let me see, you don't want the baby? Or you want the baby, just not with the man who's the father?"

She shook her head. "It ain't that, Yuseff," she sighed. "It's just crazy. I was pretending to be pregnant by the nigga Shaka just to get his paper, and now I'm pregnant by the ma'fucka fa'real. Shit wild."

"Well, what you gone do?"

"I don't know yet, I got a couple of weeks to decide."

"Well, I'm with you whatever you decide, but you know my honest opinion anyways."

"Yeah, I do. But don't tell Dajuana, at least not yet. She would flip the fuck out."

"As you wish, but what you gone do about Nikki finding out?"

"I'll cross that bridge when I come to it."

CHAPTER 17

"I'm telling y'all, I ain't even do shit," the overweight, bright skinned man said. He was dressed in a plaid shirt and jeans seated on a metal fold out chair with his hands on his knees trying to stop them from quivering.

"Hey, Mike," Officer Clue Daniels called to his partner, Mike Rutgers, who was pacing the interrogation room. Officer Daniels was seated directly across from Gully, the Flux's number one sexual predator, trying to get a read on him. Mike stopped pacing and stood to the right of Gully as he listened to his partner. Once officer Daniels had Mike's attention, he continued. "You think you could get your dick hard enough to stick in someone's ass if there was a gun pointed at you?"

Mike smiled. He and Clue had played good cop bad cop for so long that everything came natural inside interrogation. They fed off one another like a goddamn couple.

"You know what, Clue, I believe I could."

"See, I told you," Gully said with the weight of hope on his side.

"Hell yeah. I could fuck a hole through steel if someone said they'd kill me if I didn't." Gully sat back arrogantly.

"Listen," he told Clue, "the only thing is, I don't have a criminal record for fucking a hole through steel like you do for raping kids and old people"

Gully sat up in a panic and pounded one fist on top of the other saying, "I'm tellin' y'all on everything I love, dude had a gun on me and made me fuck ole girl up the ass before he made me kill her. I didn't wanna do it. Look at the tape," he pleaded.

"We have, and ain't nobody in it but you and that girl, you sick fuck." Clue was fed up with Gully. "And you keep saying ole girl like she was a nobody. She was your very own cousin, you son of a bitch."

By now Clue was up and swinging on him. Mike had to intervene.

"Stop it Clue, goddammit! Get off 'im!" Mike struggled to get hold of his partner. "I know you want him, I do too, but we can't do it like this."

By now the camera behind the glass had an edited version. "He deserves to die, Mike!" Clue kicked and ranted. "You saw the tape. The son of bitch enjoyed it."

*****

"Get the fuck downstairs," the man ordered Gully. Gully could hear the creaking of the wooden stairs beneath his feet as he descended. He couldn't see or feel where he was going because a black cloth bag covered his head and his hands were taped at the wrist behind his back.

"Where am I? What you want with me? Man, I ain't never do nothin' to nobody for you to snatch me up."

"Naw Gully, you ain't never do nothin' to nobody," the man mocked.

"How you know my name?" Gully asked, his voice quivering like a bitch.

"I know all about you, Gully," he replied, snatching the bag off Gully's head when they got to the bottom of his mama's basement.

"This my mama's house," Gully said, turning to the man who had on a Hello Kitty mask and a .38 pointed at him from his waist. "Where my mama at, man?" he asked in a panic.

"Don't worry about that, fat ass," the man said monotonously. "I have a surprise for you."

Gully's brows furrowed. "Huh? What you talking about?" The man sidestepped Gully.

"Come over here Gully," he said, walking towards the black curtain hanging on the clothesline running from wall to wall in the basement. Gully followed. The man snatched the curtain down. Behind the curtain was a gagged and naked young lady who was bound by the wrists with handcuffs and a thick rope draped over a beam in the ceiling. Her perfect titties were perky with rosy red nipples. The look of fear wasn't enough of an expression to describe the countenance on her face when the curtain came down.

Gully couldn't believe it. It was his cousin. He had secretly wanted to fuck her so bad that sometimes he jacked his dick to the thought of her. At times it became so unbearable that he would cut himself with razors or broken glass to take his mind off the sensation his dick craved to experience.

"She's my cousin, you mothafucka!" he snapped, trying to break free.

The man laughed. "Stop the bullshit. I won't participate in the foreplay of the memory you're about to create here today. I'll shoot you first."

Even though the man behind the Hello Kitty mask displayed a sick sense of humor, Gully knew that he was dead ass serious about shooting him. I guess you would call it an animal thing. Gully thought about the gun trained on him. Tears were streaming down his cousin's face.

"Why do you have me here? And why is she tied up?" The man shook his head playfully.

"Gully, Gully, Gully... Can't you see? I'm giving her to you. You've been wondering how she would feel. Now you can finally see."

"That's sick, my man."

"Not sick as you peeping into her window hiding behind the bush jacking your lil dick to her changing clothes."

Gully had that fucked up look on his face, like when a kid has shitted on himself in a corner and gets busted.

"Yeah playboy, I saw you. But I'm not here to judge. I want you to have her. Here," the man said, flipping a blade from his pocket to cut the duck tape from his wrist.

"Make your fantasies come true."

"But what if she tell them when I'm done?" The man gave Gully the knife.

"Tell what?" he said cynically. "And if you get caught later, tell them I held you at gunpoint." The man pointed to the camera on the tripod aimed at the girl. "It'll all be on tape. Even me holding you at gun point." There was a pause. They both looked at the girl whose eyes begged them not to do this. He could see Gully battling with himself and encouraged him softly with a slight hand to his lower back.

"Go ahead, she's yours."

Gully walked over to the girl and put the knife to her throat as he dropped his pants and stepped out of them.

"Okay Tiara, you might enjoy this more than me. Feel free to scream."

Her body shook in fear, the man had already killed Gully's mama and laid her inside her mattress, then made the bed back up. The police didn't find her the entire time they worked the crime scene at the house.

*****

"Would you care to sign for the package?" the delivery boy in his brown khaki jumpsuit and black boots asked Kayla, the secretary Mika hired for her new Black Wall Street company, Legit Swindle. Why people would want to trust their hard-earned drug money to a company with such a name was beyond working class comprehension.

"Sure," she answered sweetly, taking the plastic pen from his hand to sign the electronic board.

"Thank you," he smiled at her dark blue eyes, handing her the manila envelope.

"No, thank you," she replied with a smile, pushing a lock of blonde hair behind her ear.

When both these shy ma'fuckas parted, she took the flight of stairs to Mika's office and dropped off the package.

"Get that for me, Yuseff," Mika asked him politely from behind her desk. He rose from his seat to retrieve the envelope.

"Thank you," he said to Kayla before she said, "You're welcome," and retreated.

"Go ahead, open it," Mika said as he was coming back to his seat.

"Why me?"

"Because," Mika laughed, "What if its anthrax."

"Ha ha, that's fucked up." He opened the envelope. He poured the CD into his hand then looked inside to see if that was the last of its contents. It was.

"What you got there, bruh bruh?"

"I guess it's a DVD."

Mika reached in her desk and came out with a remote. She pushed a button and her Godard painting of olives hanging out of a Cadillac waving slid to the side to reveal her fifty-inch flat screen TV and security system hidden in the wall. "Put it in the top DVD player," she instructed. "The other ones are recorders for the security system."

"Aiight." He put the DVD in and returned to his seat. "Were you expecting this?"

"Nope. I'm anxious to see what it is though."

"I don't know Mika, shit seem crazy. Who in the fuck just sends people..."

What came across the screen shut Yuseff up mid sentence and made Mika weak. He immediately began to analyze the details on the DVD. He was looking for anything that would help him understand the why of what was being watched clear.

How Mika endured watching Tiara's rape as the DVD's appetizer and then her being stabbed repeatedly any where the knife would go was beyond comprehension. She had a more detailed DVD than what the police had. When her version of

Tiara 's murder was over, a picture of Dajuana flashed across the screen.

Yuseff got to his feet so fast that he totally forgot he was leaving Mika alone. He took the stairs down to the first floor an entire flight at a time. He had to get to his phone and locate Dajuana to make sure she was safe. Had he been thinking clearly, he could've easily used Mika's phone to call Dajuana.

After Dajuana's picture left the screen there was an encrypted voice message for Mika that said, "You won't see me comin' you black bitch." The voice was so eerie it shook Mika to the core, and she wasn't easily shaken.

Yuseff came back into Mika's office with a paranoid and exasperated look on his face. "She's not picking up Mika. I gotta go."

Mika came around the desk, scooping up her Dooney & Bourke purse. Grabbing her .45 she threw on her jacket and left.

She knew that the message at the end of the DVD wasn't meant for Dajuana. It was meant for her. They wanted Mika to know she wouldn't be able to protect Dajuana because as the person believed, she wouldn't even be able to protect herself if she couldn't see them coming. Shit was real clear. Taking people out of Mika's life one by one was a form of torture for Mika, until it was her time.

"Damn, Tiara," she said biting her lip to hold back the tears. Mika punched the dash board of Yuseff's black on black Escalade. *Any ma'fucka look at me crazy I'm bustin'. I swear on life they dead*, Mika thought with conviction.

Yuseff looked over at Mika, feeling everything she said. He asked, "Who we got beef with that's got the balls to get at us like this? Because you can believe Gully was only a pawn in this shit." As soon as he finished asking his question and giving added observations, his phone rang and Dajuana's picture appeared. He answered excitedly. "Where you at?" he demanded.

"Home."

"Why didn't you answer when I called?"

"I was in the shower. Why you pressin' me?"

"Get the strap and hold that bitch tight til I get home. I'm on my way," he said, zipping around the car in front of him.

"What's going on?" she asked, letting the bath towel drop to the floor exposing her creamy naked body. Laying the phone on the bed, she threw on some sweats and a tank top and click clacked her .357 automatic.

"Hello, hello!" Yuseff yelled into the phone. Sweat was forming on the bridge of his nose.

She put the phone back to ear. "I'm here. I'm getting ready so I wouldn't have to get ready. I know you better tell me what's goin' on."

"I will as soon as I get there. I'm ten minutes away," he informed her, darting through traffic.

"Aiight, I'm bout to take a look around real quick."

"That's my girl. On my way."

"Okay, I love you, boo."

"Love you too. I'm on my way."

Dajuana was seated on the leather sofa with her gun firly gripped and trained on the front door when Yuseff and Mika came through. As the door, open she noticed his beard as they walked in, getting up she went to him leaping into his arms, kissing him all over his face. They looking deep into each other's eyes she asked, "Now what's goin' on?"

Mika shut the door behind her after peering up and down the block.

"We think somebody put Gully up to killing Tiara," Yuseff stated bluntly. "The sick ma'fucka taped the shit and sent the DVD to Mika's office today."

Dajuana had a sad look on her face and tears formed in her ducts. She knew how much Mika loved Tiara and now it seemed she was a casualty of war. She went to Mika and they hugged each other hard. "I'm sorry, Mika."

"Me too."

The shit that slid through Dajuana's mind when Yuseff first came through the door with Mika was now a mustard seed in comparison to the situation, and she was also sorry for considering what she knew was long buried

"Did they get Gully?" she asked, waiting for either of them to answer.

"Yeah, they have him. I called around to ask had anyone seen him and some of the guys told me po-po got him earlier today," Yuseff answered.

"Well who we got beef with that could bring the drama on this level?" Dajuana asked while racking her brain for an answer.

"Shaka," Mika said.

"Shaka locked up though, right?" Dajuana asked, searching Mika's face for an answer.

"Yeah, I called to make sure on our way here."

"And you think he got that kinda reach from behind bars?"

"Only nigga he got out here who he can count on is Rydah, but Rydah ain't that mafuckin' disturbed to do the shit I seen on that fuckin' tape."

DVD, Dajuana would've corrected her had this been a different time, but now wasn't that time.

"Well, we need to touch that nigga Rydah just to be sure," Yuseff said.

Mika didn't want to war with Rydah so early into her fortune, but she knew Yuseff was right. She also knew that once she crossed this line that any future plans to maybe get back

147

with Shaka was over. They had to take the drama to Rydah, and hard because he had a team that was ready to die for him like them suicide ma'fuckas in Iraq or somewhere. Mika began to text on her phone.

Dajuana had one last question, "What the fuck y'all see on the DVD to make y'all rush over here to check on me?"

Yuseff was the one to answer. "Your face came across the screen once the murder was over. So we think the nigga behind this shit might try to pull up." Mika didn't add what was said after the picture of Dajuana flashed across the screen.

"It would be best for y'all to stay at the mansion. Security is tight and it's easier to protect everybody if we know where we are at all times." Mika said.

"So when we suppose to get at Rydah if we all gone be bunkered up and shit like some hoes?" Dajuana said, not really feeling the move of leaving her own family and comfort zone to go to Mika's for more reasons than she cared to discuss.

"I already put Loonie Tunes on it. He trackin' the nigga as we speak," Mika said.

148

CHAPTER 18

Loonie Tunes pulled up on one of the lil trap niggaz that sold dope at one of Rydah's spots. Money was a lil nigga that wanted to be a rapper outside of selling dope 25/8. Loonie Tunes recorded the nigga from time to time when he could coax him off the block and was glad he'd cuffed him because now he would be the inside man Mika needed to touch Rydah.

"Yeah my dude, I'll do that shot. Busta ass nigga be bird feedin' us on this block anyways, tryin' t' hold a nigga back, keepin fools dependent and shit, ya feel me?"

"I feel you my nigga," Loonie Tunes said, reaching in the console of his white Range Rover. He took out forty bands. "Here." He gave the stacks to Money, who was bug-eyed looking at and accepting the loot. "Spread this around to the lil homies. Y'all work for me now."

"Bet!" Money exclaimed.

"Still sell that nigga dope for now, but when its time, you niggaz know what side y'all rocking wit, right?" The look in Loonie Tunes' eyes told Money if he answered wrong, especially after taking his money, he'd be dead on the spot.

"Hell yeah," he answered assuredly. "Nigga makin' sho me and my Foes eat, we on the side of the bread, my nigga."

"No doubt." Loonie Tunes dapped the nigga. "So where that chump at now?"

"Chump left here twenty minutes ago, matter of fact. Said he was going to see his sister in the hospital. You know shorty in a coma, right?"

"Yeah."

Money put the money in his Chicago Bulls hoodie right by his strap and got out of the Range Rover. "I'll dead the nigga myself if that'll prove I'm down for the cause big homie."

Loonie Tunes laughed. "You gone move up fast, homie. I think I'ma leave that option on the table. Good lookin, young solid."

"You know it," Money said, throwing up four fingers.

*****

"Damn sis, I can't believe you still ain't woke up yet," Rydah said, standing at the side of Kiana's hospital bed holding her hand and silently praying to God that she would squeeze his hand, blink, or come out of the coma completely while he was standing there. Rydah loved his sister with all of his heart. They were all each other had after he killed their pops for raping her while he was drunk. The old man tried to explain to Rydah that the only reason he did it was because Kiana reminded him so much of his late wife (their mom), who had succumbed to cancer when Kiana was ten and Rydah was fifteen. The only reason Rydah gave the old man a proper burial after collecting the insurance money from his death was because he figured he owed him that much.

Looking at Kiana now helpless, lying in a bed hooked up to all the machines that beeped, confirmed for him how fucked up life is.

"I wish I knew the ma'fucka who was responsible for this shit, Key. I'd make them pay in such a way that God would damn me to hell nine lifetimes, I swear." He said it with so much conviction that he believed she would wake up on the spot, but she didn't.

"I love you sis. I'll be back tomorrow." He kissed her forehead and turned to leave.

*****

"Damn Consequence, look at this," Loonie Tunes said to the driver of the teal Caprice, who was his long time P.I.C. (Partner in Crime). "This nigga right here and ain't no police or nothin' around." They watched as Rydah was getting some lil Asian chic to put her number in his phone, not paying attention to his surroundings. He was at a hospital in broad daylight. Who in the hell would have nuts of steel to light him up right here? He was so confident in this that he'd left his burner inside his SUV.

"So what you gonna do, my nigga?" Consequence asked Loonie Tunes.

He put two slugs in the double-barrel shotgun and snapped it closed. "Pull right up on that nigga. Ain't no need in bullshittin'." He reached over and took Consequence' White Sox cap off his braids. "Let me get this for a minute." He pulled the cap down over his brows.

"Get right up on his ass too." He opened the car door to a crack, readying to pounce as the car crept up on Rydah and the girl.

"So let me get your number," Rydah said to the Asian chic he'd just bumped into. They had talked from the elevator to the parking lot where he pulled out his Blackberry for her to finger fuck her number into his long list of notches under the belt. He learned enough about her to know she went by the name Chyna Doll and that she was a stripper trying to pay her way through medical school.

She took his phone. "I usually don't give out my number to men I meet in elevators," she said sheepishly with an accent. Had she known all niggaz start out that way, she would have stayed in her lane and kept the last two digits of her real number a secret.

"What you drive anyways?" she asked before putting her final digits in the phone.

Now everyone knows just because he was driving something nice don't mean he gone break bread. Just like a dumn bitch!

"I'm pushing that new gray Yukon Denali with the Cadillac kit sittin' on eights right over there," he boasted, pointing to his whip while pushing the button to disable the alarm to show her it was indeed his car. "Wave hi, Chyna. I think she want that ass in her seats."

Chyna waved and finished putting her real number in his phone once her materialistic thirst had been quenched. "Nice." She handed him his phone back."

"Make sure you call me."

"You know I will," he said, feeling like the man after having his ego stroked by Chyna.

Yeah, bitch, I'm fuckin' you tonight, he thought, licking his lips. He had never had eggroll pussy so he was genuinely geeked. That is until they parted ways and he saw a teal colored Caprice pull up in front of him. Déjà vu ... He'd seen this moment before he could put it all together, a man in a White Sox cap was out of the car with a double barrel shotgun aimed straight at his chest. Smiling, he thought, *Damn, got caught slippin'.*

The look on Rydah's face to Loonie Tunes was almost like the nigga was welcoming death. The first boom ripped a hole in Rydah's side so huge his guts fell out. Instinctively he tried to pick his intestines up off the ground and put them back in. The second boom shot Rydah in his right shoulder and he went down. The Asian chic let out a horrific scream that would chill to the bone anyone who heard her. Loonie Tunes jumped back in the car and Consequence let the rubber burn.

CHAPTER 19

Tiara homegoing was on a Saturday, the angels were crying for her, the sky opened up and their tears blessed the Earth. Leaving the burial site with Tiara's mom, Mika and her team were headed back to their respective vehicles when a girl approached Mika and Tiara's mom nonchalantly.

"Tiara's funeral wuz-tha-bomb, y'all put it together ..." But before she could get the rest of her thought out, Mika's palm came crashing down across her face.

"Don't you ever!" Mika scorned the youngster who was probably from Tiara's high school. They all left the girl standing there holding her cheek, obviously embarrassed.

"What I say?" she called at their backs. "What I say?" But her cries fell on deaf ears.

It had been a week since that day and the streets were quiet. Nobody even tried to ride for Rydah's demise. Yuseff felt like it was Rydah who was behind the camera pulling the strings when Tiara was killed by Gully, and was convinced enough to move him and Dajuana back into their home. Mika wasn't so sure it was Rydah. The video just wasn't his style.

"You do know y'all ain't imposing on my space, right? Because this bitch big enough for y'all to stay forever," Mika told Yuseff as her butler loaded the last of their belongings into

Blood Stone

the yellow Hummer H2 that she purchased for the butler and maids to get around in.

"Thanks Mika, but shit cool."

"So it seems," she pouted, kicking a stone with her foot.

"Don't even try to lay no guilt trip on me," he laughed.

"You know we cool. I'll lay this whole city down for us to live. You know that." Mika hugged Yuseff hard. "You just be careful."

Dajuana was coming down the steps of the front of the mansion fixing her belt. She saw the embrace her man and Mika shared and became a little jealous knowing their history, but if she trusted her friend a hundred percent, she would've known that Mika really did find Yuseff a better friend than lover. Her fucking him the first time was a mistake. She fucked him a second time to make sure.

"What you doing, Mika? You know we cool and all, but I don't share my dick."

"Bitch please," Mika laughed as they dapped then slapped five three times.

"Yeah, um-hmm..."

"Anyways bitch, y'all just make sure y'all come ready to party tonight."

"I hear you on that, but you forgetting something?" Yuseff asked, looking at her midsection skeptically.

Mika totally ignored the latter of what he said. "Even you, Yuseff. You gotta let go with me tonight. Let security deal with the drama if it comes our way. That's what they get paid for. I want us all to get scummy." Then Mika looked at Dajuana. "Or as you white folks say, shit faced."

"Ya heard," Dajuana said, high fiving Mika.

"Aiight, you got me," Yuseff said, "but just this once."

"Yes!" Mika said, pulling her fist down and lifting her knee up.

That shit was hilarious and had Dajuana cracking the fuck up.

*****

That night Mika and Nikki were dressed to the nines. Mika was glad Nikki finally decided to leave her night job. She was a boss bitch now and needed to act accordingly.

She tried to reason it to Mika in a way she would understand. "I love the rush of the hustle." But it fell on deaf ears.

"You penny pinchin' bitch, we're rich," Mika countered. By the way Nikki lowered her eyes she didn't appreciate the comment. "I'm sorry, ma, that came out wrong."

"No it didn't. Compared to what I make on a daily fuckin' with you, I need to think on a grander scale." She smiled up at Mika. "That's why I bought the club from T-Bill last week."

Mika's smile was broad and radiant. "You a lie."

"Real shit. But he only agreed because I promised to shake my ass til all his shit was packed and his paperwork was in order."

"So when were you gonna tell me?"

"I'm tellin' you now." Mika hugged Nikki.

"Now that you play Monopoly, we gotta celebrate."

"You always lookin' for a reason to celebrate," Nikki teased. However, before any bottles could be popped, Tiara was murdered and funeral arrangements had to be made. That was a week ago. Tonight they would let down their long silky manes and kick it in Nikki's club, the one she renamed Sex and Bullets.

"I love that name," Mika said, adjusting her white lace Victoria's Secret body gown that hung to her ankles with deep splits up both sides of her legs ending at her waist. She had on a white thong underneath and two large white stars over her nipples. Her red gladiator sandals with pencil thin six-inch heels set her swag the fuck off.

"I know, right?" Nikki said vainly, checking herself beside Mika in the full wall mirror. She wore a red Jenna Leigh that covered just enough of her ass and titties that she had to tug at the bottom with every move. She had a long yellow silk scarf tied around her waist and a pair of shiny dark green Mauri six-inch gators on her feet with the open toes. She tugged at her bottom then stood with her hands on her hips. She stuck her leg out, forming the letter K.

"We some bad bitches."

"Yes we are."

"You look so good Mika, I could just eat you up and say fuck the club."

"You the one looking like a candy bar." They laughed.

"Let's go."

On the ride over Mika asked about Salomon.

"Oh, he still calls me actually."

Mika's brows furrowed. "Oh, fa'real?"

"You said that like my pussy bunk, Mommia. Don't get it twisted," she said, pursing her lips and rolling her eyes.

"Girl please, I just thought you ....you know...."

"He was typical?"

"Yeah."

"He is," Nikki said comically. "And he payin' like they typically do, too."

"That's what's up."

"Want me to move over there with him too."

Mika bit down on her lip and the rest of the ride to the club was rode in silence. That was with the exception of Marsha Ambrosius stroking the sound system.

They pulled up in front of Sex and Bullets in Mika's brand new smoke gray Double R sports car on black metallic twenty-inch rims. Before the valet could come over to open their doors, hard hitters on Mika's team had gotten out of three black on black bullet proof Escalades, one in front and two in the back, and let them out. Ten men, who looked like black ninja turtles, exited the cars. Six went in with Mika and Nikki and the other four posted up outside by the vehicles. Onlookers in the long line, mostly bitches in skimpy shit trying to be overly cute in the chilly night air, were thinking the women who just waltzed in the club must be major as fuck because they had been standing outside for forty-five minutes and those hoes just waltzed straight in. Fuck!

Inside the entrance of the club was another door with a stairwell behind it that led to the hallway where Nikki's office and VIP rooms were located. Some shit only the mafia were privileged enough to be seated in, it cost $100,000 a night. This was an exclusive privilege. Later on only three people were VIP enough to have a sit down while the club was juxing, but there were a chosen few also who paid to have sit downs while the club was closed.

Puffy had partied with his people. 50 Cent did his thing, and Teyana Taylor spent $500,000 on her birthday to throw a circus party, landing in the middle of the street in a helicopter with her crew.

The club was so packed that night the building's bricks had stretch marks on them to prove it.

The thing that made the VIP room so special, besides the tight security, bulletproof tinted sliding glass wall overlooking the dance floor, the fully stocked bar, private stage, KFC kitchen with walk up window, and the world's most sexiest bitches whose pussies smelled like water ready to give it up to the special guests, was the fact that no electronic device would survive the radio waves the walls emitted to kill wiretapping and bugs, which made the room trap proof on a federal level. No watches with hidden cameras; no cell phones; and no wire transmittal. Safe! Was it worth the money? Nikki's clients thought so.

To make sure everything was on the up and up, each time the Mob went in to do what they do, a burn out cell phone was taken pass the threshold to make sure it would die instantaneously. It wasn't that Nikki's clients didn't trust her, they didn't trust anybody, and they damn sure weren't gonna rely on some shit that could fail, so they checked the room each time as a precaution. But there was a switch that could turn the power off to the system so that people could chill on a regular night if they wanted to, and tonight the system was off.

Nikki got her phone and called down to Missy, who oversaw the bar, and asked her to bring up a bottle of Ecstasy, Blue Dolphins and Naked Ladies, to be specific, and a quarter pound of purple haze. With the phone between her shoulder and ear while she mixed a Long Island Ice Tea, Missy told the caller, "I'm glad y'all finally made it, girl. I'll bring it right up."

"Thanks, and put Satin on the stage. Her ass gone get this bitch all the way live."

"Here you go, sweetie," Missy said to her customer, handing him the drink. He immediately slid it to his lady friend on the left after he paid Missy. "I'll do that now and be right back up," she said, putting the money in her apron.

A knock came at the door of the VIP room. "Either this bitch straight outta Marvel Comics or this one of our peoples," Mika said, answering the door with unflinching confidence because there was an army an enemy had to get through to get to the door.

Dajuana had dyed her hair fire red and had it in a French bun with two sparkling gold spiral bangs framing her beautifully painted face. Her attire for the night was a mint green colored, rose laced pullover nighty made to look like a Polo shirt that she wore like a skirt. She had on a nude colored rose lace bra and matching booty shorts on underneath. On her feet were mint green Mauri crocodile pointy toe three-inch heels.

Mika had to step back to check her out. "You have got to be the prettiest white bitch in the world, and if you ain't you'll do til' that bitch get here. She done shut my shit down," she giggled.

Nikki saw Dajuana when Mika stepped to the side.

"Damn, bitch, you just got off didn't you...Looking like Poison Ivy from Batman."

Dajuana put her hand on her hip and strutted her way through the door. "Bitch, I do this er'day...Ya heard!" she boasted, putting a dip in her right hip.

Mika and Nikki both laughed.

"Where my big brother at hoe," she asked, popping her gum loudly.

"Right here," Yuseff said. Turning his attention from the security he was talking to, he stepped behind Dajuana.

Turning around Mika spat, "Why you ain't get all muslimfied on her ass and tell her to take that shit off?" She walked over and gave Yuseff a tight hug.

Yuseff was a 6'3 caramel snickers bar thugged out in all black.

"Well, she said y'all was gone be dressed the same way so I didn't wanna spoil y'all swag thing," he joked, ending their embrace.

"Plus, she pouted... Shid that's how she got me," he laughed.

"So the bitch cheated is what you're saying?" Mika teased, popping her gum.

Dajuana and Yuseff both let out a laugh.

"Whateva!" Dajuana teased, waving Mika off.

Just then the DJ announced, "And to the stage for your viewing pleasure and mind, get yo muthafuckin' dollars out as we welcome Street Consequence's finest model ever and my future ex- wife...Sat-tin!" The strobe lights danced wildly and stopped as the spotlight shined on Satin. The crowd went wild as she made her way through the club dressed as a naughty nurse.

Gliding up the ramp onto the stage, she made sure her hips swerved left and right to the beat of Gucci Mane's "Freaky Girl." Once Satin got to the stage, she smoothly dipped it low. Her voluptuous mocha cheeks pushed the skimpy white skirt up, showing a peek of her whole ass. Twerking her cheek muscles left then right, her ass jumped and all the ballers in attendance started making it rain all over the stage.

Loonie Tunes came through the door of the club with Mary on his arm. Security checked them and his thugged out entourage. Once in the club the group separated, strategically blending into the crowd in case something jumped off. They all had certain points in the club covered, but to the untrained eye, they were just there to party and have a good time. Loonie Tunes was wide open when it came to Mary. Nobody could testify that they had ever seen him sporting any other chick on his arm like this.

"Wuz up wit this jungle fever shit niggaz is on now days," one of the sistahs in the club spat as they walked past her.

"Shid, another baller taken off the market by some white bitch. Fuck is this shit," her friend said, rolling her neck as she shook her head.

A waitress headed up the spiral staircase from the dance floor that led to the VIP room. Two guards were posted up at the door with twin Glock .40s on their hips.

Just then Loonie Tunes and his lady approached the VIP door as well. Looking at the monitors Nikki hit the remote button and the two bullet proof sheets of glass slid open, allowing the group to enter. The entire team greeted the couple as they stepped onto the red-carpeted balcony with shiny brass railings. She spoke to everyone and started taking orders for the bar then headed back downstairs.

Just then, the glass doors slid open and Mika, Nikki and Dajuana danced their way into VIP. The money started hitting the floor like a hailstorm. There were about six inches of money layered all over the floor. Mika and her crew smiled from ear to ear as they entertained their adoring fans.

One dude sat at the bar throwing back shots, unimpressed by the show they were giving. With a fiendish look on his face he thought about what he came there to do. *Tic Toc Tic Toc*, he thought with a devilish smile, tasting himself before rising out of his chair.

Mika look over at him with a raised eyebrow. There was something about the way he walked that gave her an eerie feeling. *That nigga looks familiar*, she thought, squinting her eyes. As she tried to focus in on his face he had already made it to the exit and was gone.

When the club finally closed and the last of the partygoers were gone, Mika and her crew were fucked up. Yuseff and Loonie Tunes got the ladies together and headed out to the vehicles. Since Mika and Nikki were both wasted, Loonie Tunes drove them home in Mika's car while Mary tailed them in his Range Rover in between the security detail.

Yuseff, on the other hand, never really cared for security. He didn't really feel the need to draw that kind of attention to himself but wouldn't hesitate to annihilate any ma'fucka that tried him. Dajuana rode in the passenger seat knocked out as Yuseff looked over at her pretty face, mouth wide open and drooling. He smiled and thought, *three am, the witching hour.*

The streets were desolate and it seemed as if Yuseff was catching every green light. Out of nowhere, a purple box Chevy slammed into the side of his Lexus truck so hard it almost flipped in the middle of the intersection. Before Yuseff could even think, another one slammed into the other side of his truck, causing it to jump up on the curb and into a pole. His head lolled to the side and he could hardly breathe. Reaching over to check on Dajuana, he noticed her head was against the windshield. All Yuseff saw was blood running down her face like a heavy red rain.

Just then two armed men ran up on his truck, swinging open the doors. One of the men snatched Dajuana out, handing her off to a third member wearing a Hello Kitty mask.

Both gunmen riddled Yuseff and his truck with AK-47 bullets; his body jerked and danced with every shot. Multiple shots chipped at his head until it looked like a bloody puzzle piece.

CHAPTER 20

Loonie Tunes and Brick were making rounds to all of
Rydah's old trap houses to collect the money and give the new
workers their re-up. Loonie Tunes was more comfortable in this
game than washing dope money and illegal surveillance. He
really couldn't get with that, although his breaking and entering
skills were on some Mission Impossible type shit.

Loonie Tunes and Mika used to set up wiretaps and
cameras in government officials' offices, homes and businesses
so she could get enough damaging information to extort them,
and if need be, call in a favor. She recorded a call that exposed
the Mayor and Governor being on the down low. She recorded
the Governor calling the Mayor behind his wife's back to talk
about how he missed him blowing his asshole out. Mika used
to wonder how their wives could be so gullible. Overall, it
wasn't a bad hustle. Loonie Tunes just felt he took to the streets
like a fish to water because he was a street nigga, not some
wanna be corporate underboss trying to come up with a grand
scheme to take over the world. This wasn't some movie or
novel he was trying to live out. In his real world, you ruled one
block at a time, baby.

"Yo, why that bitch Mika got all that money and wanna be
on some crooked shit? Don't she know all any nigga out here

wanna do is be able to leave this shit alone? Shit crazy," Money contemplated, thinking how stupid Mika was in his mind.

"She know that shit," Loonie Tunes stated, pulling over to the curb in front of a lime green trap house trimmed in white, his last drop off.

"She just wants the power to go with the money she got. You can't keep what you got if ma'fuckas don't fear you, feel me?"

"That makes sense," Brick answered, having seen what Mika was on in a whole other light. He opened the car door and stepped out, walking into the trap house to take care of their business.

Loonie Tunes got ready to leave out and put his lieutenant Powder outside. They called him Powder because he was an albino kid with pink eyes and gold hair.

"Keep your ear to the street. If you niggaz hear anything about Dajuana or who took my mans Yuseff out, hit my hip ASAP."

"That's money, big homie," he said humbly, his eyes twitching from his condition.

*****

"Y'all ain't got no word on Dajuana?" Mika asked as soon as Loonie Tunes and Brick came through the door of the VIP room.

"Not shit yet," Loonie Tunes said, taking his black leather Pelle Pelle off and tossing it on the red leather sofa.

"Me and my niggaz got our ears to the streets though, Mika," Brick added. "Somethin' gone shake, that's my word." His Brooklyn accent came through on the backend of the words he spoke.

"Yuseff's funeral is in a couple of days," Mika said, flopping down on the sofa hard. Her eyes were puffy and her stress lines were in full bloom across her forehead. "It seems like I'm burying my whole fuckin' team," she said gravely.

"Whoever this is has to be dealt with immediately." She laid her head back and closed her eyes.

"Why can't we just enjoy this money and live happy? God!"

A knock came to the door of the club. Mika looked around to see if anyone was expecting a guest of some sort, but the head shakes and shoulder hunches let her know that this knock was an unexpected one. Mika and her team, with the exception of Nikki, all pulled their straps, heading down the spiral stairs. They crossed the dance floor. Loonie Tunes snatched the door open. Daylight poured in over the mail courier shining light into the club like daybreak in a dark cave. Loonie Tunes snatched him in, pinning him to the inside doorframe. He stuck his head out of the door, looked both ways, and shut daylight out. Everybody had their guns trained on the mail courier. Mika took off his ball cap with his business logo on it and put her .45 Bulldog to his temple. He shook violently, causing Loonie Tunes to use more muscle just to hold him and pat him down.

"Clean!" Loonie Tunes spoke, training his 9mm on the center of the trespasser's face as he gave him some space.

"Who the fuck is you," Mika barked as Brick relieved him of the manila folder. Mika snatched the folder from Brick, pushing it in the mail courier's face.

"Who the fuck sent yo muthafuckin ass ... What the fuck is this?" Loonie Tunes spat.

"I don't know!" The mail courier's voice quivered.

"The fuck you mean you don't know?" Mika questioned.

"I was on my route and one of the city's traffic control center employees asked me to drop it off and gave me twenty bucks. I was told to make sure I gave it to Mika," he said. "Oh, he said if you doubt my words to tell Mika don't hate on his fox head."

"You know who this nigga talking about Mika?" Loonie Tunes asked, still pointing his gun at the courier's face.

Mika laughed. She knew exactly who sent the package. It came from a nigga named Choice.

"Let that square nigga go," she waved, walking over to the bar.

"What," Loonie Tunes asked as a creased formed on his forehead. He looked back at Mika then at the courier and wanted to know what was going on.

"Lower ya shit, my nigga," she spoke, touching her .45 to his .9 in a lowering motion. Money hesitantly followed suit, standing a safe distance away just in case.

"So who the fuck this nigga, Mika?" Loonie Tunes questioned.

"Choice," she answered, leaving it at that.

Mika thought about how in love Choice was with her back in the day. But she could not get into a square ass working type nigga and decided to leave Choice hanging because Nickel was getting money at the time. She opened the envelope and pulled out a CD.

"What's on this," she questioned, tipping her head to the side. "I swear I don't know," the courier spoke with fear in his eyes. "Alright." Mika sighed, throwing her head back. "Let dat nigga go, he don't know shit."

Loonie Tunes reluctantly opened the door and let the man out, closing the door behind him.

How we suppose to watch this shit? I ain't got no damn VCR, Mika thought, causing a crease to form on her forehead.

After spending a day hunting down a VCR, Mika, Nikki, Loonie Tunes and Crazy Dough sat in the VIP room watching the tape. The crew was in amazement as they watched Yuseff's murder and Dajuana's kidnapping. Mika shifted in her seat to get a clear look at the third person on the tape. Even though the person was wearing a mask, his walk caught her attention.

"Muthafuca," she grunted.

There was no mistaking that walk. It was very distinctive because of the limp and with a closer look she could see braids that were tucked inside the person's collar. There were not too many people in the Flux that could coincidentally have both characteristics. But was what she did warrant enough to kill? And why bring Tiara and Dajuana into it?

"Yo, y'all niggaz see this ... This shit is crazy," she said leaning forward.

"You know who did this don't you?" Loonie Tunes asked, seeing a glint of recognition of who grabbed Dajuana.

"Yeah," she said as she got up from her seat. "Yo, Crazy Dough."

"Wuz up sis," he replied.

"I want you and yo dudes to bring that clown ass nigga Bogus to me," she instructed.

"Bogus? Aw, hell yeah. I gotchu," he replied, grabbing his nine and heading out. Halfway down the hallway he doubled back, peeking his head in the back of the room.

"Aye Loonie, I need a ride big homie."

CHAPTER 21

Dajuana was hanging from the chains bolted into the beams that ran the length of the ceiling of the barn. She was badly beaten and sweating profusely. Hay and grass clung to her stripped flesh and bloody skin. Her toes were teased, barely feeling the straw on the ground beneath them. Bogus had taken her fifty miles outside the city to put this lick down. There was not a house or highway for miles and miles. He pulled his dark blue Jeep Cherokee inside the barn and boarded its massive doors. No one could save Dajuana. With no tower signal, Bogus wouldn't be disturbed and the crafty work he planned for her would last as long as he wished.

She thought he would have finished her off last night, but he hadn't. On the inside, she prayed for her torment to end, but on the outside she was numb. Soon it would be over. She was looking forward to death. Dajuana was weak, beaten, and broken. Her teeth were loosened something awful. She found herself pushing against them with her tongue like piano keys. She wasn't gonna beg Bogus to kill her. She managed a weak laugh.

"You like to laugh, huh?" Bogus asked sarcastically. "Like you did when you sent that picture of my mouth around the city." He stalked around her hanging weak body, putting on potato peeling gloves.

174

Her lips creased the corners of her mouth. "Shit was pretty funny."

He slapped her body hard with his gloved hand and scraped her soft skin like she had slid across the unforgiving concrete.

"Agghhh, you bitch," she said through cracked dry lips.

It would've been hard for anyone else to understand when she talked to Bogus, but he understood her slurred speech completely. It turned him on.

He slapped her again and again. "I should knock your teef out bitch. You wanna run around, you and that bitch Mika, like y'all the shit, but," he slapped her lower back, causing her to scream something God awful, "I'm the shit bitch. Me, not you, me."

Dajuana's eyes were swollen almost completely shut, but she could make out the silhouette of the man she saw grabbing the rope overhead getting ready to swing down.

Bogus was so amped up that he didn't notice they hadn't been alone since last night. The man who'd followed him back here after the kidnapping didn't require the food and water necessary to sustain human life. He had been trained to do without for long periods of time while he waited and listened. When Bogus turned his back and he had acquired Intel to satisfy himself, he sprang into action. He swung down on a rope and kicked Bogus in the back, knocking him over. Bogus quickly rolled over to see who had taken him by surprise. His eyes bugged out of his head.

"You're not supposed to be here."

The man walked over to Bogus, grabbed his head between both hands. Lifting him up he broke his neck then dropped him like a sack of potatoes. He went to Dajuana and freed her.

"Why are you saving me?"

"Vengeance is not his," he said.

CHAPTER 22

"Do you know who I am?" the man asked, washing Dajuana's wounds with a soft sponge in a house he had purchased for his business while he was in town. She was lying in bed being nursed back to health by unfamiliar hands.

"Yes...Shaka," she answered. "Where am I?"

"Safe." Shaka said.

There were footsteps coming up the wooden stairs that Dajuana could hear. Her senses had become very heightened since being hurt.

"Who's here with us?" she wanted to know desperately.

When the door opened she was in awe. Was her blurred vision lying to her?

"There are no need for words, Dajuana," Shaka said.

"What the fuck is this? You got a twin, my nigga?"

"Yeah, Daku is my brother from Africa. While you bitches were plottin' to steal money from me, I was making a family connection."

Dajuana looked back and forth between them.

"Crazy huh? I'm still gettin' used to this shit."

"Mika don't know you out, huh?"

"Nope."

"So what you gone do with me then? If you ain't let her know you out by now, then you don't want her to know. So you gotta keep me quiet."

"Smart."

Dajuana looked at Daku.

"That's what you meant when you said vengeance is not his."

"You should rest," was all he said.

When Daku took Shaka by the arm and led him just outside the room, four of Daku's rebels marched in, two stood by the walls and two by the windows. A fragile black woman scampered in behind them. She was the nurse helping to put Dajuana back together.

"So what is your plan brother?" Daku asked Shaka.

Shaka looked Daku in his eyes.

"Entirely or with her?"

Daku tossed his head towards the bedroom door.

"Let's start with her."

"I will make her trust and love me. I have no beef with her. She is only doing what any bitch would do if their friend came into some money. If she chooses not to love me, then I will hack her into catfish bait."

"And what of the bitch, Mika?"

"I want to make her pay like no one has ever paid, and then kill her. Simple."

"Well, we need to get this done quickly. We have business to attend back home."

"How long do I have to handle this shit?"

"By tomorrow night. Then we must go."

"Damn, that's soon," Shaka said, thinking real hard.

"Do you need more time?"

"I would think so."

"So you do not intend to march in, kill everyone, and leave out?"

"Hell naw, I wanna see the bitch suffer."

"Fine," Daku said. "Take my men and do what you must. It is your affair, but when we get to Africa and it comes to my business, I'll show you how to kill. When we finish, you will have a body count the devil will be proud of."

Then Daku left in his BMW 6-Series. Shaka returned to the room where the nurse was taking Dajuana's vitals. He sat down in the chair next to her bed.

"Damn Dajuana, dude did a number on you."

She actually tried to smile.

"Tell your brother I want to thank him for what he did."

"I will."

"My teeth and gums hurt like shit," she said, then ran her tongue over them.

"I'll have a dentist come in to fix you up once you start to feel better."

"Why are you helping me? I feel like you're fattening up the turkey before the feast."

Shaka took Dajuana by the hand and held it so close in his that she could feel his dick rise through his touch. Whatever he was about to say she was sure he meant it.

"Dajuana, I'm sorry about Yuseff. He wasn't a bad type nigga."

Dajuana began trying to get out of bed.

"I gotta go," she was in a panic. Tears spilled down her face.

Gently Shaka held her in bed. The nurse moved aside.

"Hold on, Dajuana. Where you goin'?" he asked her in a concerned tone. At this point he was just that. She lay back reluctantly, smashing the bottom of her fist on the bed once then repeatedly from the frustration she felt. Shaka's aim was to calm her down so he spoke softly when he addressed the matter.

"I know what a loss this is for you. Believe me." He looked her in the eyes; a soul piercing stare.

"His funeral is in a couple of days but I can't let you go."

"To hell if I'm not! That's my man."

"Come on, Dajuana, you got to think. Bogus' team is gonna be heated. He's gone and they're gonna want their lick back. They know they can catch Mika and everybody else at the funeral. If I was trying to hit 'em up for some shit they did to me, that's what I would do. So for your safety, I gotta keep you here."

"But Mika and them didn't kill Bogus, you did." As soon as she said the words she immediately wished she could take them back.

"I'm sorry. That came out wrong. I guess I should be grateful."

Shaka sat down in his seat. He became solemn.

"Don't trip. The thing is, it don't matter who killed him. All that matters is that you escaped Bogus somehow and they gonna assume Mika had her hand in it."

"But why do you care? By now you know Mika fucked you outta all your bread. Don't you want your lick back too?"

The look on his face said it all. Dajuana had her answer. But asking the question was easy. Swallowing the truth was hard.

"I'm gonna kill Mika, no doubt. But my beef ain't with her squad, unless they make it to be. That's why I want you to lay back. You don't have to die with her. You have a choice. What's done to Yuseff is done and Mika made her own bed. What you do is on you. No one is stopping you. If you want to get up and walk out of here, you can." He pointed. "There's the door."

Dajuana thought back to the day Shaka came in and rescued her and Mika. "How did it get to this," she asked more herself than to Shaka. "You know she pregnant don't you?"

"Yeah, you mean how she tricked me into believing she was with whatever she had in her shirt," he said feeling heated.

"Not that, Shaka. I mean like she really pregnant. She told Yuseff you got her pregnant for real when y'all did it in the county. Nobody supposed to know. Not even me, but she is."

Shaka got to his feet. He wasn't even gonna address what Dajuana was talking about. Fuck Mika. "So by you laying in bed, I take it your choice is made?"

"Would you really kill me, Shaka?"

"You know there was a time when it was suppose to be me and you, but you gave us up because you thought Mika loved me."

"What are you talking about, Shaka?"

"You asked how did it come to this. Had you chose me then, we wouldn't be here now," he said, then left the room. "Nobody in or out," he told Stone, who stayed behind to make sure the rebels were on their square.

"Enough said," Stone told him.

"You know, Shaka, Daku is like a brother to me and I will protect him with my own life as I would you because that is the bond we share. I know this news of him having a twin brother and coming to America to discover you is true...well there's a lot on his mind. Let's be done with these low life people and get back to Mother Africa. You are the heir to a mighty throne. There are way more pressing matters than the ones you face here, dealing with a no good bitch."

They stood face to face. Shaka took all of this in, but he could never see the real picture until he stepped foot in Africa.

"All this time," he began, "I knew there was more to my life than this." Shaka thought about what Ciara had once told him, *you mother sent you here so that you could live.*

"There are so many questions I need answered," he said humbly.

Stone put a hand on his shoulder. "As soon as you're done here, Daku will start to answer what he can. He is on the same mission. Mine is to make sure you both see completion, and I'll die doing it." Shaka took a stroll after the brief conversations he had with Dajuana and Stone. He decided not to spray Yuseff's funeral.

CHAPTER 23

The same black BMW 6-Series that was seen in the video of Yuseff's murder and Dajuana's kidnapping was now slowly cruising here at Yuseff's funeral. *What's the connection*, Mika wondered, turning back as his mother tossed a handful of dirt onto his ivory and gold casket. The Benz backed up and left when everyone started to disperse.

Although Mika couldn't see the man's face behind the tinted windows of the limousine, they had made eye contact.

Later that night Mika was laid back resting her mind when she got a call from Loonie Tunes.

"Yep," she answered disinterestedly.

"Yo, what's up?" He sounded excited.

"My mans just hit me up talking about they ran a short news clip talkin' about they found that nigga Bogus dead as a motherfucker in some barn fifty miles out in a town called Freeda."

Mika sat up. "Bullshit!"

"Nah, straight up. And guess what else?"

"Talk about it."

"Somebody else was there with him chained up, but now that person missin'."

"Dajuana..."

"Great minds think alike. I got my people checking out the same leads the police got. If I hear something, you gone know cuz somebody gone be dead."

"Get at me."

"I got you. My word, we gone get at any ma'fucka cross us."

"No doubt."

Mika hung up the phone. She knew Dajuana was out there, but where? Her mind was working overtime. She had to get her girl back.

Two months had passed and there was no word about Dajuana, but the search was still on. During that time the only body to turn up stankin' was Crucial. Shaka had reluctantly laid low but had to make sure that when he struck that he could strike hard and effectively. During his down time, Daku suggested he train his body and mind to endure pain with a ninja master from Japan living in Brazil. Now he was back with a disciplined mind. He knew he would need one because before he realized it, there were errors in his judgment.

CHAPTER 24

"You're not suppose to be out for another month," Bruce said to Shaka as he entered his home through the front door and saw him sitting on the sofa in his living room. There was a sense of urgency in his voice.

"Where's my family," he asked hurriedly.

"They're upstairs."

"What?" he said, about to break in a full sprint up the stairs to get to his wife and kids.

Shaka said, "You don't wanna do that."

"What have you done to my family? I swear to God..."

"You swear to God what?" Shaka seethed, feeling his anger rise to the occasion.

"What your bitch ass gonna do?"

Bruce got some act right after seeing the blood in Shaka's expression, and decided to see what Shaka wanted with him. He decided to calm down.

"Okay, Bryce, are they okay?"

"Yeah, they straight. A lil tied up but they cool."

"So what is it that you want with me?"

"It's quite simple actually," Shaka said with a bright smile.

Bruce knew as a lawyer that a smiling snake was the worse kind. Whatever Bryce had up his sleeve Bruce knew that it was a lot worse than simple. "I'm listening," he said while loosening his blue and pink striped necktie. He went to sit on the sofa to appear more confident than he really felt on the inside. Inside he was shaking like a bitch and only took the seat so Shaka wouldn't see his knees knocking like a ma'fucka.

"I just want you to call Mika and set up a meeting, that's all."

Bruce looked apprehensively at Shaka, then to the phone and back to Shaka.

"That's it?"

"That's it," Shaka said sincerely.

In the closet was one of the three ninja assassins that Shaka brought with him from Brazil. He exited when Bruce picked up the phone, and crept up behind him, wrapping the black test line in his leather-gloved fist.

"I don't know why I'm making this call when I know you're gonna kill me once I do."

Shaka sat back and laughed.

"You really don't know me that well, Bruce. I would never kill a family man. That's not how I roll."

Bruce pushed Mika's number in and waited for her to answer.

"Hello," Mika answered skeptically because she didn't recognize the number.

"Bryce is here in my house..."

The man standing behind him worked fast and had the black line around his neck cutting through the meat of his neck like hot butter. Bruce dropped the phone and scratched and clawed at his neck, trying to get a finger or fingernail under the line cutting off his life supply of oxygen. His eyes were as big as bo-dollars as he struggled. He kicked his feet wildly, knocking over the coffee table and sofa pillows as he was pulled over the back of the sofa.

"Hey Bruce," Shaka called teasingly.

"I told you I wouldn't kill a family man, but my mans chokin' you out, he just don't give a fuck my nigga."

Shaka picked up the phone with Mika still on the other end and said, "I'll be t' see you in a minute, bitch," and hung up before she could get a word out.

Shaka then got on his phone and said three words, "Light it up."

*****

"Hello! Hello? Bruce! Answer me! Brucc!"

She could hear him struggling in the background. *Shaka,* she thought, as fear came over her. Could he really be out? Hell naw. "Bruce!"

Then she heard all she needed to confirm her worst nightmare, Shaka's voice. If she still had any doubt about it really being him, it was squashed.

"I'll be t' see you in a minute, bitch."

Mika couldn't even recover from her shock before choppers were cutting down her mansion. She hit the floor and covered her head. Where in the fuck were her guards? She crawled to the living room closet and slapped a hundred round clip in her modified M16 with grenade launcher, took some extra clips then went to a part of her wall that didn't resemble Swiss cheese. She began firing through her windows at an enemy she couldn't see. Clack Clack Clack BOOM! Clack Clack Clack BOOM! The front yard looked like a war zone.

Trained assassins with machetes had killed most of her guards while she was in the shower, unable to watch her security monitors. Now she regretted not putting them on her shower walls. Nikki said she was overboard already with them in the ceiling above the bed so she chilled and now look. She had her back against the wall for ten minutes, exchanging gunfire. Seven empty clips lay in front of her before the exchange came to a complete halt. She took a chance getting to the shattered window only to see the rebels walking off her compound as if from just another day at the office. *Who in the fuck is them niggaz, Africans*, she wondered. That nigga plugged with them people for real and I got his money. Stupid, stupid, stupid, she cursed herself. I gotta get outta here.

Mika didn't have to bother with packing luggage. Once she made it to the cellar and to the hidden underground passage behind the wine shelf there was a duffle bag with her bare essentials in it, a sweat suit with Air Max ACGs and two Berettas and $100,000 cash. She took her robe off, dropping it to the floor and threw on the sweats. She held one Berretta in her hand and the other stayed in the bag. Mika walked the lamp lit tunnel for about a mile then climbed the ladder and pushed the lid aside. She was inside a garage that stored her black Dodge Charger. She got the hidden key from underneath the car, opened the door, and tossed her duffle bag with the money in the back seat. The Berretta stayed in her lap.

"Your girl is very clever," Stone told Shaka as he watched her Charger leave the garage a mile away from the warzone.

"I taught that bitch well," Shaka sneered proudly.

Stone pulled in behind her but stayed a comfortable distance back.

CHAPTER 25

"Stupid, stupid, stupid!" Mika slapped the steering wheel, berating herself for getting caught off guard. All the fucking surveillance and I can't even watch my own house.

"Fuck!" she screamed. "I can't deal with this shit right now."

Mika checked her rearview mirror. After seeing nothing suspicious, she got off the city streets and onto the expressway, not knowing this would help Stone blend in even more.

She couldn't trust her own phone so she tossed it out the window. All she needed was her guns, money, and a place to get herself together. She really didn't have a thought out plan or destination until she tossed her phone. She should've called ahead to let her granny know she was coming through, but didn't wanna chance giving someone the heads up via radio signal. She knew all about how sloppy phones were and was hell bent on not letting counter surveillance be the death of her.

Mika hit a few blocks just to be sure she didn't have a tail. But little did she know, once Stone saw the familiar landmarks of the neighborhood that Mika had led him to that he would take a chance on her going to her grandmother's home and parked his car a block away. He had been here with the private investigator who not only gave him Mika's entire rundown before Shaka got out, but showed him every person close to her.

Later he returned by himself to learn the streets. All of this
information was cross-checked with Shaka to make sure he
minimized all fuck ups. He and Daku didn't have time for it.
They needed to be getting back to Africa to handle family
business.

"Teepical," Stone said as he watched Mika pull in front of
the garage of the small white single floor house with trim and
began to unload her things, which wasn't much.

She had the duffle bag in one hand and her Beretta in the
other. If anybody thought she wouldn't go out in a blaze of fire
running up on her, they had another thing coming. Her
grandmother opened the door to her home and held open the
screen door before Mika could pull it open and ring the
doorbell.

Her grandmother had big gray curls that had been set with
the largest rollers. Her teeny reading glasses were hanging on to
the tip of her chocolate round nose. She had on a pink rayon
and silk shirt with a blue and yellow pattern on it, too big sweat
pants covered her big mama legs and pink house shoes with a
blue and yellow flower stitched in the middle of them the size
of a nickel covered her black stocking socks.

Mika didn't try to conceal her weapon. She and her granny
had a very open relationship. Ever since Mika was sixteen, her
granny instilled in her to never lie to her no matter how painful

the truth. "Always give it to me in the raw," Ms. Della used to tell her. "Now, tell me what happened."

Mika remembered that was the first time she confided in anyone about her mama's boyfriend Charles, and from that day forth, she felt comfortable telling her granny anything.

What I haven't told you yet is that the reverend Esko J, granny's piece of dick, was an ex con convicted of armed robbery and second-degree murder. He was ordained as a Christian priest while doing his stint to convince the board to grant his parole. While on lock he met an old Irish man who promised him very large amounts of money if he could pull off contract kills for his Irish mob on the outside. Only they would never meet the killer. He would set up everything and Esko J would deal directly with him and that's it.

Sebastian, the Irishman, never knew when he would have to contract his own mob and didn't want them to see it coming, so he said nothing. Esko J went home to Ms. Della when he got out. She was the only woman to hold him down his entire eight years, but to keep her safe, he'd only see her when it was convenient to take her to places like Bermuda, Korea, London, and Africa, when he had to make good on a contract. No one at the church knew that Ms. Della was the love of Esko J's life because over the years they became better friends than lovers and it was easy to conceal their relationship.

When Ms. Della told Esko J about Charles and what he'd done, no one ever heard of Charles again, but by this time her grandbaby was long sold and if Cheryl wasn't her own daughter, she would've had her indirectly killed also and turned a blind eye. Mika was her favorite granddaughter and she almost lost her to the bullshit they put her through. My baby in the streets pimped out. The thought made her cry her soul clean. All she could do was praise the young man who brought her baby back to her.

"What's your name, baby?" she asked.

"Shaka."

"Shaka, I like that. You hungry?"

And now Mika was running back to granny like she always did. Call it instincts. When granny saw the gun she was cool with that. It's better to have it and not need it than it is to need it and not have it. But as a woman of the Christian faith she felt it was her duty to tell Mika, "Vengeance is mine … saith the Lord."

"I know Granny, but this black ass is mine and I gotta protect it," Mika said, following Ms. Della into the house.

"I hear you," she said to Mika as she turned to go into the kitchen to pull her cornbread out the oven.

"So what happened?"

"Damn Granny, I don't know where this shit start."

"Just start at the beginning," she said, putting the hot cornbread on the stove next to her fried cabbage and corned beef. She took her mitts off and sat down.

Mika recanted everything to Ms. Della, not leaving out one detail. Ms. Della shook her head.

"One thing I know, Shamica," she began, "You can mess with a man's clothes, you can mess with his car sometimes," she giggled, "but you can never play with his heart and you never fuck with his money. You did both of the nevers when he was already down." Ms. Della shook her head again, feeling the weight of Mika's burdens.

"So what you suggest I do, granny?"

Ms. Della patted Mika's knee.

"I suggest you eat and feed my great grandbaby."

Mika rose to her feet. "How did you know?"

"Come on, I know everything." She took Mika by the hand, letting love move them.

By now Shaka was sitting with Stone in his car and two of the rebels were inside Ms. Della's house. There were no dogs barking in the neighborhood, which allowed the rebels to go in the window of Ms. Della's bedroom in the back of the house undetected. With no alarm system, getting inside quietly was even easier. They eased out of the bedroom with a machete in one hand and a Glock .17 in the other. In the hallway they could hear the women talking and advanced towards the voices.

"How long the boy Shaka been out?" Ms. Della asked, fixing Mika's plate.

"I don't know, but he knew where I lived..."

Then it dawned on Mika. It was stupid for her to come here. She turned on the ball of her feet.

"Come on, granny. I gotta get you outta here. I never shoulda come here, I wasn't thinking."

"Instincts child."

"Let's go, granny!"

But it was too late. She felt the barrel of the gun pressed to the back of her head and her Beretta being taken out of her hand.

"Easy child, you don't wanna go making a mess of things."

The other man had his gun in Ms. Della's back, leading her away from the stove and to a seat at the table. He slid his machete into its nylon sheath on his side. There was a roll of duct tape that dangled on his opposite hip from a clip and he tossed it to his comrade.

"Here."

He caught the tape then sat Mika down to be tied up.

"Well aren't you gonna tie the older lady down," he asked in his native African tongue while securing Mika.

"No. She poses no threat. Plus, I was given specific orders not to touch her."

With that said, he got on his mobile and called Stone. Mika thought about trying to bribe the two Africans, but thought about how much money the nigga leading them must have. Instead she pleaded with them to let her grandmother go when Shaka strolled in through the front door with the grace of a king dressed in all black.

Without a word he walked over to Mika and slapped her hard across her face. She tried to speak and when she did he came down hard across her face again with his open palm.

Ms. Della couldn't take it and jumped to her feet.

"You stop it right now! You stop it, Shaka!" she yelled at him as one of the African rebels put his arms around her to restrain her.

Shaka met her eyes. "I'm quite sure by now you know your sweet innocent grandbaby tried to play the shit outta me, huh Ms. Della?"

She didn't answer. Shaka smiled.

"Yeah, course you do," he said and slapped Mika again, snapping her head back.

Mika laughed at Shaka and said, "Oh, wook at da wittle bitch have a temper tantrum."

Shaka smiled. "Speaking of babies..." he lifted her sweatshirt and saw the bulge in her stomach and the black line running from her naval disappearing into her sweats.

"So you are pregnant."

"Yep nigga and it ain't yours, bitch ass…"

"For your sake, you better hope it is," he cut her off.

It dawned on Mika that he hadn't intended to kill her. Of course not because he could've did that at the mansion.

"So what do you want, Shaka? Your money back?"

"Nope," he said slyly, then told the rebel holding Ms. Della to bring her to him.

"What are you doing Shaka?"

Mika bucked against her restraints. The chair jerked but the duct tape had no give in it. Shaka took two halves of the double barrel shotgun from his back pocket and put them together, then loaded it, snapping it closed.

"Shaka," she struggled. "Shaka, what the fuck are you doing?"

Ms. Della was standing in front of Shaka facing Mika. She smiled.

"It's gonna be okay, Shamica. God…"

BOOM!!!

The double barrel was so loud when it went off that it seemed to shake the entire earth. Shaka was ruthless, but Mika didn't know the extent of just how ruthless until this nigga blew her grandmother's head off with a double barrel shotgun. Blood, brain, and bone painted and peppered the family pictures on the wall behind her grapefruit pink and red. Mika fought against the duct tape restraints binding her to the chair.

She was completely helpless. One of Shaka's goons stood behind her, forcing her to look at his boss' gruesome display of revenge. Mika made threats but Shaka's damage had been done and there was no taking it back. A single tear escaped Mika's eye and trailed down her swollen, bruised cheek when her grandmother's headless body hit the floor with a dry thud and began to jerk violently. This wasn't the first time she had been a witness to death. Lord knows she put in much work with this nigga back in the day. But this was different on a whole other level. This was her grandmother. An innocent. A woman who had devoted her entire life to the neighborhood church and the raising of the whole hood.

There wasn't a child or adult who didn't know and love some Ms. Della. And if the corrupted soul in this nigga could be so cold and callous as to turn her grandmother's head into potted meat, she could only imagine what he had in store for her. But being the boss bitch that she was, she refused to beg a bitch nigga like Shaka for her life. Mika squared her shoulders back and was ready to take her dome call like a real bitch.

"Kill me, bitch ass nigga!" she spat with venom, hoping at that very moment that he would make good on her demand so that he could end the pain her heart was enduring.

Shaka turned to Mika and smirked. He kneeled down in front of her, propped on his toes and passed the sawed off to one of his henchmen to the right of him.

"Now why would I do that?" he asked cynically. "When that would defeat the purpose of you feeling my wrath upon your life?"

He stood to his full height of six feet, two inches.

"Let's go," he commanded his two henchmen, and they casually walked out the front door just as smoothly as they had walked in.

Mika turned her head away from the deadly scene of her grandmother lying on the floor in a pool of blood in front of her. She let her head dip low for a moment of silence, then lifted it with a renewed strength and made a promise aloud. She would get her revenge on Shaka and she would serve it to him cold.

She looked down at her granny's hand real close and saw that there was a faint red light blinking on a medical alert looking thing. Mika didn't know that before Ms. Della was killed she had paged Esko J. He gave her a pager to contact him in case of dire emergencies.

When the red light on Esko J's wedding ring flashed and he felt it shock him, he put his 745 BMW in reverse and pulled out of his driveway. Checking his glove compartment, he pulled out his .357 revolver and checked the chambers.

CHAPTER 26

"So you decided to let her live, brother?" Daku asked Shaka in the backseat of the Benz as Stone drove them all to the private airstrip to be lifted off in the G6 and carried back to Africa. The rebels followed close in five black Hummers. They would stay behind to establish a market for the diamonds they were gonna send back to build a dynasty with the American dollar. Shaka had already made up his mind that he was returning. While he was gone though, they would train with the ninjas to be equally ready with the use of objects around them as they were with their guns and machetes. With the real rebels and ninjas in place, he could return to an army without having to build one. Money would take care of the rest.

"I'll make her suffer so much that she'll beg for death and welcome it with a thank you when I'm done with her," Shaka said.

"A queen bee survives is enough to build a new hive," Daku said, leaving Shaka puzzled somewhat. "But she does have our blood line in her womb."

"We're here," Stone said.

"Thank you, my friend," Daku said.

"So you gonna tell me about how all of this shit kicked off, finally? Or are you gonna keep speaking in riddles of wisdom til I figure our history out on my own?" Shaka asked impatiently.

Blood Stone

Daku touched his leg. "On the plane brother." He had to laugh. "There's a long journey ahead of us and before we land in Mother Africa, you will know everything I know. From there we will be putting the rest together, together brother."

*****

Rahmi opened the door for him when the car stopped in front of the hangar. Daku hugged him with love. When Shaka stepped out and Rahmi embraced him.

"Ain't you one of the rebels that was at the house when I put the old lady to rest?"

"Yes," Rahmi answered.

Daku stepped in. "Rahmi, this my twin brother, Shaka. Shaka, this is my brother Rahmi."

"Why you ain't say shit when we was at the house?" Shaka asked him.

"I wasn't there to talk. I needed to know that you had the heart for war...and you do," Rahmi answered.

"Let's go brothers," Daku said, then turned to Shaka. "Are you sure it was wise to send that white woman to Africa for mating?"

"Hell yeah, bruh. I heard y'all African ma'fuckas got AIDS over there like a ma'fucka."

Stone laughed hard.

202

"He thinks he's not African. The American black in him is stupid."

Everyone laughed but Shaka as they boarded the plane. The rebels were scattered aboard with AK-47s angled across their chests in their hands waiting, almost begging, for some action. The ninjas disappeared from sight.

*****

There were too many men for Esko J to handle when he drove past Ms. Della's crib nonchalantly. He saw seven men in black total. Esko J knew that whatever happened in the house death was involved because he recognized the three of them, the man in the middle from his travels to Africa.

"Daku's rebels, why are they here?" he said out loud. Could it be revenge for killing Kenya? But how could they have figured out my connection to Ms. Della? He was ambivalent as fuck. He knew the answer would be better answered if he followed them, so he hit a block knowing the men hadn't paid him any mind then followed the black brigade when they left.

They made a few stops then headed to an elusive airport. He took a dirt road on the side and put his foot on the gas. Once he was on the hilltop, he got out of his car, hit the trunk and took out his sniper rifle. He took aim at the cars on the tarmac where they had gathered with the Hummers.

Looking through his scope, he could see two Dakus. *What the fuck is going on?* He thought as he watched the men board the plane and take off. He knew that shit was deeper than he could handle because he knew the history of the two men on the plane, Daku and Stone. Stone was the reason he had the long scar down his face. He wanted to take him out right then but shit would've been too sloppy. He regretted having to get back in his car without spilling any blood, but he had to if he wanted to kill every one of the men he'd just seen fly away.

In his car he knew he had to go see Beno. He was the master assassin, the one who mobs talked about like the boogieman because no one had ever seen him and lived to tell about it. But Esko J knew exactly who the man was personally and where he could find him. But first he had to go back by Ms. Della's to see what damage had been done.

*****

"Daku is on his way back and he has your other son with him," Abdu informed the group of three in the room with him.

"Good, very good."

"There will be a war when they get here, so prepare yourselves," he said, and the room stood on edge.

CHAPTER 27

"I just came across a lick on some new product for the low," Consequence told Loonie Tunes on the phone.

"Fa'sho," Loonie Tunes replied eagerly, checking his rearview. He was pushing his white on white Range Rover through heavy traffic in the Flux.

"I'll be to see you in a minute."

"No doubt," Consequence ended the call.

"Now let my son go, my nigga, he just a shorty. This grown man business."

Shaka was inside Consequence' apartment in the North Loop Projects where he lived with his baby mama, Chantel, and his one-year-old son, Cartel Jr. Two highly skilled ninjas had their katana blades on either side of his neck while he was on his knees beside the corpse of Chantel. She had been killed by two Chinese men who threw stars to her face to let Consequence know that they didn't come to his house to bullshit.

He tried to be a hero when the door first flew open and smoke quickly filled the tiny living room. With his gun in his hand, he fired once blindly before the Chinese star lodged in his hand between his knuckles and made him drop his .380 to the ground. He took hold of his hand and winced in pain. When he saw the star between his knuckles, he couldn't believe it. The movies had come to life in his living room. He took the four-point dagger from his hand and threw it to the floor. Before he could think of his next move, bone-crushing kicks to his ribs, neck, and kneecap made him crumble and the katana blades kept him there.

He was hurt so bad by the contact sport of the ninja that he couldn't even hold his hands up in surrender. When the smoke cleared, Chantel lay lifeless with a Chinese star embedded deep inside her forehead and one through the bridge of her nose and Shaka had one of Cartel Jr.'s tiny hands in his. He wanted to buck but he knew he was out classed. Pride wouldn't allow him to jeopardize the life of his son.

"What you niggaz want?" he asked, trying to fight the pain coursing through his body.

"You have a partner named Loonie Tunes." It wasn't a question.

Shaka squeezed Cartel Jr.'s hand and the little boy's lip trembled as he clawed at Shaka's hand to release his. "Right?"

The ninja applied pressure to the blade's edge when Consequence tried to move.

"Yeah, yeah, man." Tears filled his eyes. "Let my son go, man. What he got to do with this?"

Shaka loosened the boy's hand but still held on to it.

"Daddy? Daddy?" Cartel Jr. begged for Consequence.

"Mommy?" he cried, looking at his mommy while not understanding why she wasn't coming to the aid of his cry.

"Do you fully understand the gravity of this situation here?" Shaka asked.

"I would if I knew what the fuck was going on," Consequence said, probing for a simple answer.

"You can at least give me that much before y'all off a nigga."

He knew the business. Don't no nigga put in work without a mask on unless he wasn't leaving behind no witnesses.

Shaka breathed deeply, then exhaled slow.

"A couple of months ago you and your people killed a brother of mine while he was at the hospital visiting his sister."

Consequence' forehead grew deep wrinkles. "Man, I ain't have shit to do with that!"

Shaka squeezed his son's hand as he clawed at his and jumped around like he had to pee really bad.

"You drove the fuckin' car. Then you drove the fuckin' car off with ya mans after he took my brother out."

Consequence wanted to go to his son.

"Daddy! Daddy! Daddy! Hurt Daddy. Hurt! Oww...Oww..." he whimpered.

"Come on, homie, let my son ride. What you niggaz want? Is it money? I got two hundred thou under the floorboard in the room. You can have that if you just leave."

"Fuck yo money, nigga. Do it look like I came here because I'm hurtin'?"

Consequence was quiet. Shaka just looked at him and thought, *I'm taking the money anyway.*

"Get Loonie Tunes over here and I'll let your son live. If not, I'm going to kill your son in front of you so that you know in Hell that he didn't make it, you feel me?"

"Yeah, I got you my nigga."

"Well, get him here," he demanded with a hard jerk to his son's arm.

"Aiight, aiight," he cried. "Got damn man, I ain't know shit about your brother."

"Well, now you do, and it's time you niggaz paid the Consequence, huh?"

Consequence didn't find it funny having one of his murder lines used on him before his own death. He placed the call to Loonie Tunes, giving him the impression that he had a good thing going to get him there fast. Consequence hoped that Loonie Tunes was G enough to peep the play that was going on at his spot and dead the niggaz in it.

"He's on his way, now let my son go, my nigga."

*****

Smoke, Zae, Cheese Burger, and Danielle sat on a picnic table in front of building 1013 in the North Loop Projects choking on a blunt when Loonie Tunes approached.

"What up, niggaz?" he said.

"Not shit," Cheese Burger, the fat dark skinned kid with his rusty feet inside some thin ass flip flops said.

"Was tryin' to see where that gunshot came from a few minutes ago," Danielle said, pulling on the blunt. She was the pretty yellow bone who stayed fighting bitches because of her complexion.

"Pass the blunt bitch, before I have Shaneeka come out here and fuck you up," Zae told her, throwing his dreads back.

"Get you and that bitch shot...and fuck you nigga, who you callin' a bitch? Yo saggy titty mama a bitch. With that raggedy ass apron she got on."

Loonie Tunes and all the fellas laughed. All of them thinking about Zae mama really having long, flat titties and always wearing that old tattered duster so that the neighborhood kids could get a peek of her long nipples hoping that some horny ass teenage boy would find it in himself to mercy fuck her silly without her son finding out. Who the fuck even wore dusters anymore anyways? Most kids didn't even know what they were. Zae didn't find it funny and was about to address that shit with Danielle in a real fucked up way, but Loonie Tunes asked more about the gunshot to lighten the mood.

"And nobody out here got hit?" he asked, making a sweeping gesture with his hand over the project layout.

"It prolly wasn't shit," Cheese Burger said. "You know how it is out here. Some ma'fucka prolly just popped off to let it be known he got a thumper."

"Yeah, could be," Loonie Tunes said, then strolled off.

"Y'all be easy."

"You too, bruh bruh," Danielle said.

"And don't think I'ma let that shit you said about my mama slide," Zae told Danielle.

"Ay Cheese," Danielle said with a devilish grin.

Cheese Burger laughed when he answered because he could tell her calling his name was a set up for a punch line. They'd all been around each other long enough to see this shit coming.

"What's up baby gurl?"

"What Zae mama cookin' if her titties hangin' in the skillet?"

Cheese Burger was cracking up and hadn't even heard the line yet.

"I don't know, what?"

"Fried bologna sandwiches."

Smoke, who normally kept his composure when his homies got to ribbing each other, doubled over in laughter. He had fucked Zae's mama on the low and remembered her titties, but having someone else confirm that them shits was long and flat in Zae's face was the funniest shit he had ever heard in his life. Zae upped his burner.

"Keep on talkin' that shit bitch, and I'ma fry your got damn bologna," he said, then laughed.

"You's a stupid ma'fucka, Danielle." He snatched the blunt from her hand.

"Gimme this mafuckin' blunt. Now talk about my mama titties again and I'ma fuck you up," he said, laughing at the joke while thinking he didn't have a good enough come back to get the last laugh.

Loonie Tunes was laughing hella hard at the group of four when he entered the building, they group stayed bugging out.

A chick named Karla was coming up the block and heard all of the laughter. She thought they were talking about her. She couldn't stand Danielle and found this to be an opportune time to start shit because she had her girls, Cindy and Tina, with her.

"What's up bitch?" Karla barked. "You poppin' off?"

"Fuck you talkin' to?" Danielle said, ready for whatever.

"You bitch. What's good?"

"Don't even trip, Danielle," Zae told her.

"That bitch run over here and I'ma knock huh ass out. I been wantin' her brother to come wit it since his punk ass been home."

"Nah, homeboy, I got this." Danielle squared up.

"What's up?"

Loonie Tunes' mind was back on the matter at hand as he took the eight flights of stairs up to Consequence's pad. He was praying that Consequence came across a way better price than the twenty-seven thousand they were paying for each brick. Shit was way too high but what could a nigga do if he wasn't willing to hit the highway himself? If they could get 'em at twenty-two stacks each, he'd take ten to twenty, but as high as they were now, all he wanted was six at a time. The shit they were getting was still decent enough to put a fifty on and hit it with the mixer, but it took too long to get off.

He better have some good news or—

*****

Loonie Tunes had done enough B&E's to recognize that shit wasn't what it was supposed to be from the few splinters he saw worked out by the door knob. Plus the hallway didn't smell of Chantel's Jasmine scented incense. Instead it smelled like sulfur and fear.

He took the two pieces of his sawed off double barrel shotgun from his back pockets and put them together. Gunshot was the word that came roaring to his mind. He hoped that nothing happened to his main man and had it been anyone else, he woulda caught the news. He put his hand on the doorknob and gave it a twist, then put his hand back on the shotgun. The door creaked open easily and eerily. He gave it a nudge with his foot. He didn't call Consequence name because he didn't want to alert anyone of his presence. Never in a million years would he have believed Consequence would set him up to get fucked off and that belief is what allowed him to venture further into the apartment.

Loonie Tunes was looking all around but never once looked up. Over the doorsill balancing himself with the use of the ceiling and small feet, the ninja waited like an owl on a branch as he watched his prey grow more confident and bolder. He dropped to the floor quieter than a pin falling into cotton and held his sword above his head, ready to strike. He had already lifted his mask when he thought about the trap his victim would be walking into and as he stood behind Loonie Tunes, he fixed the dart in his mouth perfectly so when he blew it out; it would hit its mark with precision.

The slightest miscalculation and he would have cut the man's head off instead of paralyzing him. The ninja blew the dart from his lips like a whisper and it stuck in precisely the right nerve in the back of Loonie Tune's neck, shutting his mobile skills down instantly. All he felt was a pinch with the bite force of a mosquito and didn't know why his body shut down.

Loonie Tunes grunted and tried to push forward, but nothing happened. The ninja appeared in front of him and relieved him of his shotgun.

"Who the fuck are you and why the fuck you look like a mafuckin' ninja?" is what Loonie Tunes wanted to ask. This some fucked up shit I done walked my ass into. Robbers? But why me?

Shaka came from the back room where the ninja had Consequence captive. He had Cartel Jr. by the hand. "I'll take that," he said to the ninja. The ninja handed him the shotgun. He inspected it and said, "This the same one you killed my brother with?"

Loonie Tunes was trying to talk with eye movement and mumbles. Then he saw Chantel's head with the Chinese stars in it sticking from behind the couch. The stars were embedded in her face so that no blood oozed from the wounds.

Shaka smiled.

"Oh, you can't talk." He paced around Loonie Tunes.

"Well, let me make it simple for you. You killed my brother, Rydah. I know you didn't think that shit was gonna go unpunished? Now what I'm thinkin' is that bitch Mika put you up to do her dirty work since you fucks with the bitch like that." Shaka laughed vainly. "That bitch shoulda gamed yo ass about me in the process."

Shaka put a hand over his heart and said sincerely, "Personally, I'm offended." Shaka and Cartel stopped pacing and stood in front of Loonie Tunes. "Why that bitch tell you to kill my brother?"

Loonie Tunes couldn't convey with his eyes that Mika sent a fucked up hit out on the wrong ma'fucka and that it shoulda been his ass that she sent him to kill.

"Don't matter. He dead now and that's a fact."

Shaka said something in Japanese and the ninja brought Consequence out with the sword to his throat.

"I'm sorry bruh, they was gonna kill my son," Consequence pleaded. Loonie Tunes was murdering Consequence with his eyes.

Shaka lifted Cartel Jr. by his arm then tossing him in the air, he caught the little kid by his small head and swung him hard, like a baseball bat, breaking his neck. It was so quick no one even saw it coming.

"Nnno-oooo!" Consequence yelled out horrifically, making an amazing leap. He tried to run for Shaka with his hands out but the ninja cut his head off with one clean swing of his sword. His head hit the floor like a heavy weight. Blood spewed out of his neck like a water fountain as his shoulders jerked. Consequence eyes were wide open when his head hit the floor.

His last sight was of his little Cartel being tossed to the side like a rag doll and his body falling to the floor doing the catfish flop.

Shaka kicked Consequence' head up the hallway. "Bitch ass nigga." Shaka laughed. "When I came in here today, I knew heads were gonna roll."He finished laughing then became serious again.

"That's one disloyal nigga. He knew he was done and called his mans up to go down with him too. If that ain't some fuck shit. I never woulda done that," Shaka said, shaking his head. He looked at Loonie Tunes with apathy.

"That's why I killed his son. Can't have a bloodline like that on the loose to mate. Might get with a real bitch and fuck her line up, ya feel me? How a real nigga like you get caught up with that fuck nigga anyways?"

Loonie Tunes was thinking the same thing.

"Anyways man, the girl at the strip club said that my brotha was trying to put his guts back in when you shot him again and took his life."

So that's how he knows I killed his brother. Chyna Doll. Big mouth bitch! I knew I shoulda killed that hollering bitch when I had the chance.

Shaka traded one of the ninjas the shotgun for his sword. Loonie Tunes could only look in horror and mumble incoherently. Shaka put his hand to his ear.

216

"You say somethin? Oh, I see...what we have here is a failure to communicate." Shaka lifted the sword. "Well, let's fix that. Let's see if you can put your guts back in."

Shaka held the sword with expertise and brought it across Loonie Tunes' stomach swiftly. All of his insides fell out of him like chain link hotdogs and blood. Shaka then took the dart out of his neck to allow him a chance to put his guts back in before he and the ninja disappeared.

*****

"I was wondering why, after all the training you endured in Brazil, you had a shotgun to use on the old lady?" Rahmi asked.

"They took something from me with it so I took something from them with it," Shaka said blankly, looking out the window of the G6 at the white clouds that he would probably see again if he took the time to look up when they were settled in Africa.

"Well, you don't need it now, brother," Daku said mildly.

"And why did you kill the kid?" Daku was curious. He would never kill a child unless there was no other way.

"I didn't want the little bastard to grow up and kick my cane from under me."

Daku knew that his brother was a menace and decided that he would have to keep a close watch on him. Even though he was his twin, he was still a stranger.

"Well, I guess I better tell you how me and Rahmi became brothers and how you ended up in the United States."

"What about everything else?" Shaka wanted to know.

"I'll answer what I can and after that, the rest is still to come."

Shaka sat up and Stone and Rahmi paid attention as well. They didn't want to miss a single beat of this story. Though Rahmi knew most of it, he was amped up as if it were his very first time.

"Start from the very beginning, Daku. I wanna know erthang..."

Something behind the glint in Shaka's eyes put Rahmi on point. He didn't know what it was, but he wasn't gonna overlook it. Overlooking shit is what gets you killed.

CHAPTER 28

Esko J made it back to Ms. Della's house only to find her headless corpse and Mika duct taped to a chair overlooking her. He placed his .357 revolver in his lower back and rushed to free Mika.

"What the fuck happened here?" He knew that he was going to find death here when he saw the three ninjas and Daku and his rebels leaving the house. Now he had a witness who could help him to understand why they had come, and why they chose to kill his heart when they killed Ms. Della, and why they left Mika living.

Mika rubbed her wrist once the tape was off and took the liberty to undo her legs that were taped tight to the base of the chair.

Esko J relieved Ms. Della of the pager in her hand and shut it off. As soon as he did the red light in his ring stopped flashing. He lifted the pretty pink throw fabric from the sofa and covered Ms. Della's body with it while he mourned silently.

Mika came over and sat beside him with tears in her eyes. With his head down he addressed Mika. "I asked you what happened here, and don't bullshit me."

"The long version or the short version?" she asked.

He looked to his left at her.

"The long version because I need to know why men from another country would take an interest in coming to America to cause mayhem, kill a woman like Ms. Della here, and leave you alive taped to a chair. So, like I said, don't bullshit me."

"You saw them?" she asked, wondering why he hadn't done anything if he had.

He acknowledged her question with a nod of his head. "Now tell me what I need to know."

Mika took a deep breath. "It all started when my girlfriend Nikki got at me bragging about her meeting some niggaz from Africa who owned some diamond mines."

"Do you know their names?" he asked patiently.

Mika looked back into her head. "The one she fucked with was named Salomon and his guy was Lewis, I think."

"Was that it? Do you know if there were more than that?"

"There were but she never mentioned their names. They went to the West Coast to take care of some shit out that way."

"Okay. Did you ever meet the two men she came to know?"

"No."

"Aiight, continue," he said, confirming that she never saw anyone but the ones who came today.

"Well, to let Nikki know how serious he was, the one named Salomon gave Nikki a diamond worth some serious paper, but come to find out the reason they were here in the first place was to locate the heir to one of the big men who died in Africa who had a huge stake in the diamond mines."

"I take it you knew who the person was," Esko J said with an accusatory tone.

"Knew him?" she said excitedly. "He was my ex boyfriend Shaka. Imagine me finding out this nigga who used to play the shit outta me was fixin' to be caked the fuck up and I wasn't gonna get my chunk because I left him in jail...Shiiid, so I played his ass. I married him in jail and had him sign over all his legal shit to me."

"Which was?"

"A hundred fifty million dollars. That's how much they were buying him out to never come to Africa and get in their way."

"Did he know that before he signed over his money to you?"

"Nah, he didn't know nothing because I just told him they were power of attorney papers so that I could handle stuff for us while he gone."

Esko J was furious. He could kill Mika himself.

"So Ms. Della lay here because your ass was chasing a fuckin' dollar? Gaming some nigga because you felt he owed you?" He got to his feet so fast and snatched Mika by her arm she could've suffered from whiplash. Both of his hands were on her arms as he shook her.

"Money, Mika? Are you fucking serious?" he screamed.

Mika didn't think of it that way until Esko J made sense of it in that light. Now she was even more hurt and wished she could take it all back. He released her.

"Jesus, Mika."

He rubbed his hands over his salt and pepper hair as he paced the living room. Mika only watched and felt guilty that this was all her fault. Trying to play a game with the big dogs and really didn't know how.

"Do you even know who that boy Shaka's family is and how serious this shit fixin' to get? My God, Mika, what the fuck have you done?"

"I'm sorry, I didn't know."

"Answer me this, why did these people let you live?"

Mika rubbed her stomach. "Because I'm pregnant with Shaka's child."

"You better hope that's enough," he said, stalking out of the house.

Esko J was dressed in a plain white shirt, faded jeans, and sandals. It didn't matter that he had just left forty degree weather because where he was headed the sun was still shining bright. He knew Mika's story had holes in it, but the gut of what he needed to know was clear. The root of all this evil was money. Something else he knew was that whoever came to see

Shaka didn't come with Daku and had no clue that Daku was Shaka's twin brother and also heir to the same share in the diamond mines, which made the contract Shaka signed void. Had they known this vital Intel, Esko J was quite sure they would've tried to kill Daku before buying Shaka off. They had counted on Shaka's Americanized ways to sell his heritage up shit's creek without a paddle for money.

The plot was interesting to Esko J, but he wasn't on the plane to head a private investigation into the family background of the notorious Daku and his newly found kin and their inheritances. He was on the plane to go find the world's most elusive hit man and ask for his help. Though Beno owed him a favor, he didn't want that to be his angle when dealing with him, because what he did for Beno was from his heart and that's how it would stay. If Beno chose not to help him, he would just go at it alone.

The good thing about taking this time to think was he still had the element of surprise on his side. Mika confirmed that Ms. Della didn't die because Stone had finally found out where the man who killed his precious Kenya had started his life over and came to get even. He did that coincidentally while at the same time waking up a beast who had been asleep for years now. Esko J was now back on the trail and would finish the fight between them once and for all.

Esko J's flight landed him in one of India's oldest and holiest cities, Jodhpur. The sun was so bright he had to shield his eyes when he got off the plane. There were men with turbans on and dark bob haircuts loitering around the airport holding signs for the foreigners who needed guides to make it through their city. The atmosphere was very humble, welcoming, and trusting; something Esko J could never get used to. He looked around the crowd until he spotted the oldest looking man in the bunch and went to him. The man put on a broad crooked smile and shook Esko J's hand while saying something in Hindi. The man's eyes were darting around Esko J. He was wondering if he had brought luggage or maybe had misplace it. Seeing this to be the old man's dilemma, Esko J said, while using his hands, "No, no, no. No luggage. I travel light."

The old man flashed his broad crooked smile again and said, "Oh, have you?"

Esko J felt a little better having a guide who could at least speak English.

"Yes," Esko J said. "You speak English?"

"Little," the man said. He threw his sign into the trunk and headed to the driver seat.

"Come on." Taking Esko J's hand, he indicted for him to sit in the front seat beside him.

"Thank you." Esko J took the seat and they left the airport.

224

Once they cleared the airport the old man introduced himself with a much friendlier handshake and said, "Sheesh."

"Michael, Michael Taylor," Esko J said, giving him the name he used on his passport then released his hand.

"Strong name, like bull," Sheesh said with a smile.

Esko J didn't bring along any luggage because he wanted to purchase the proper attire worn in the country to better blend in with the culture, but he did need a nice place to stay and some of the country's fine cuisine to feed his hungry belly.

"Know of any good hotels with a kitchen?"

Sheesh pursed his lips and waved Esko J off as if to say nonsense. "Room in my house."

Esko J wanted to protest but didn't want to come off as offensive if he denied the man his extended hand and hospitality, so he sat tight.

"The wife, Nadia, cooks the best food in all of India. She comes from a long line of mothers who cooked for kings. They even prepared meals for the Kumbh Mela festival every twelve years. Her first one she was twelve. She's twenty-five now. You missed a great day by one year," Sheesh said proudly, his smile reflecting the sweetness of his memory.

Esko J thought Sheesh was at least seventy years old and here he was with a wife that was twenty-five. He laughed at the old man inwardly because he was amused by his youthful enthusiasm.

Sheesh told him all about his grandfather's goat herding lineage and how his father came into farming tobacco. He told him how he himself took on all the responsibilities and how driving a cab was one of his five jobs. This he had to do to keep all four of his wives and seventeen children with everything they needed.

When they pulled up to Sheesh's brick palace, Esko J was literally amazed. He would've thought that by the old beat up Chevy, four wives and seventeen children that the man was struggling to get by. But it was apparent by the sound structure of Sheesh's palace that all of his business ventures put him at the top of the food chain in India. Esko J was thinking that any second they would stop in front of one of the many white or blue houses clustered together in the tiny neighborhoods, but instead they were at a palace that Sheesh claimed took fourteen years and three thousand workers to complete. No doubt in Esko J's mind the claims were true.

"You have a beautiful home," Esko J complimented sincerely.

"Thank you. My first wife made me keep it in our family." Sheesh walked across the lawn barefoot, leading the way to the beautiful entrance.

"Come, come," he said. Esko J took his sandals off and followed suit.

One of Sheesh's daughters greeted him at the entrance of the palace. She was dressed in a green and gold robe type of thing with gold ropes and jewels hanging onto her forehead from a tiara. There was a see-through green veil over her face from the nose down which revealed her mysterious dark eyes. She greeted Sheesh excitedly in their native tongue then kissed him on both cheeks. He pulled away with an admiring smile.

"Zaria, this is Michael Taylor. He is an American and will be staying with us for a duration, welcome him," he told her politely.

"Nice to meet you," she said, not extending her hand to accept his outstretched one. So he quickly took his back. He forgot that no other man in this country touched a woman unless she belonged to him. That is unless the husband offered his guest the chance to fuck his wife. Which some of these people did from time to time and got offended if you turned his offer down. Esko J was hoping he would not be placed in this position.

"Nice to meet you too," Esko J said. "Your father is very kind to have opened up his home to me."

She laughed. "Sheesh is not my father, he's my husband." She giggled at Sheesh, who was beet red. "Sheesh, I like him, he's funny."

Esko J was a little embarrassed but they made him feel very welcome so he got over it quickly and stepped inside their palace. He thought that he was about to run into a whole lot of little ones when he entered their home, but that didn't happen. Most of the seventeen kids that Sheesh had were grown or off to college. The five kids, ages seven and under, he had with his last two wives, Nadia, age twenty-five, and Zaria, age nineteen, were the only ones who lived at home and they didn't run wild because his first two wives, Tamara and Luzwana, both age fifty, were raising them along with his latest wives, and they weren't having it.

With this knowledge Esko J was able to distinguish that the young lady approaching the three of them dressed in the all white robe of a dress with sparkling silver and gold trimming with a veil to match was Nadia. Her hands and feet were adorned in colorful jewels, which set her apart from Zaria. This established the status she held in Sheesh's harem of wives because Zaria had on very little adornment. Later Esko J found out that Nadia bore him all sons, four of them, and that made Sheesh hold her highest, even over his first wife, Tamara.

"Come, come," Sheesh told him, leading the way down an artful hallway.

"You can meet everyone over dinner. Right now let me show you the guest room while my wives prepare a meal."

"Thank you," Esko J said politely.

Sheesh waved him off modestly. "Come, come."

Sheesh opened the heavy door to one of many of his guest rooms for Esko J. What he saw upon entering was a great marvel. Esko J's eyes swept the room slowly from the high ceilings with the chipped and fading portraits of Sheesh's ancestors painted centuries ago on it to the marble floors. There were exquisite paintings of Cathedrals, the Kumbh Mela festivals, beautiful women bathing in the Ganges River, and many more. It's easy to say Esko J was utterly in awe of so much beauty. He almost felt guilty for being in such a lovely home with beautiful souls knowing he had the darkest intentions before him. *Is God trying to show me the life I could be living if I'd submit to him and stop using him as my cover-up to live this secret, murderous life?*

Sheesh had walked off without Esko J realizing it because he was so stunned with the layout around him. When he came shuffling back across the room with a porcelain basin filled with the sweetest smelling water, Esko J didn't know what to expect, but then he remembered.

"Come, come. Have a seat," Sheesh said, motioning for Esko J to have a seat on the huge bed with thick cream blankets and red throw pillows everywhere. Sheesh sat the water basin down.

Esko J went to have a seat and Sheesh snapped a towel and draped it over his knees. Esko J wouldn't protest although in America he wouldn't dare let another man wash his feet, but he knew it was this man's culture. When Sheesh was done he humbly walked out of the room leaving Esko J to his thoughts.

Esko J woke up bright and early the next morning planning to leave before Sheesh's family began their day. He took a quick shower and headed for the front door.

Sheesh was outside under the dark blue-black early morning sky washing his cab when he heard the door to his home close. Without looking up he asked Esko J, "Leaving so soon?"

"Yeah, I think I've over extended my stay in your lovely home by a night," he said modestly, rubbing the bulge in his six pack abs. "Anymore and I'll eat you outta house and home."

Sheesh waved his hand. "Oh nonsense," he laughed. "You're a man on a mission. I can tell. There are ants in your pants."

Esko J smiled at the outspoken wisdom of the old man and threw his hands up in surrender. "Okay, you got me."

"So where you off to?" Sheesh asked. He dipped his yellow sponge into a bucket to soap his tires.

Esko J walked over and took the other sponge from the bucket and joined Sheesh in washing his cab. "I came here to look for an old friend."

"I take it he's an American like you?"

"Yeah."

"What's the young man's name?"

Esko J made circular motions with his sponge over the trunk.

"I doubt that you know him."

Sheesh stood.

"Son, you see this?" he asked, waving his hands wanting Esko J to see the vastness of the land. "This is Sheesh's country. I know everyone in India as I know India. Now, what's the name of the man you seek?"

Esko J started to let it go to save Sheesh face, but what the hell, he had nothing to lose.

"His name is Basheer, but I call him Beno."

Sheesh frowned as if checking his mental database to see if the name would register. Then he said, "Mr. Basheer..." Sheesh laughed. "I owe him one on the chessboard. Very clever man."

Esko J couldn't believe it. "You know him?"

"Sure do," Sheesh said.

His eyebrows came together as he said, "He won't tell me what those three dots inside the flame behind his ear means, even if I promised him three wishes." He hunched. "One day..."

The old man really does know his country and everyone in it, Esko J thought.

"When can you take me to him?"

"Take you to him?" Sheesh asked with a hint of humor in his tone.

"Yeah."

"After breakfast." He tossed the sponge into the bucket.

"Come, come." He took Esko J by the arm.

CHAPTER 29

1988

"With the King of Egypt, Asu Rah, trying to move in on our land so that he can control the diamond trade to fund illegal wars, my father thinks that it's best that our Tanzanian army join forces with Angola," Zebadiah was telling Kaleah.

"But Asu has plenty of diamonds," she pleaded.

Zebadiah got to his feet and ran his rough dirty hand over his nappy head, something he did when he was stressed. He began to pace the small study in his father's mansion.

"I know this. The man's just not content with the diamonds that wash up river for his workers to pick over. He wants the mines that produce the blood of Africa. His lands are not as rich as ours in East Africa."

"Does he know that your father only has twenty-five percent take in the Tanzanian mines, and the rest is for the Europeans who have bought into the industry?"

Zebadiah waved his hand dismissively at her question, as if it didn't matter.

"Tanzania only has twenty-five percent of the mines the government knows about. We have bigger and better mines that we own privately. Since World War II we haven't put our true wealth on the market."

"So what does your father do with all the money he gets from harvesting these secret diamonds?"

"We want all of Africa back up to what she is supposed to be, but...."

"But what?" she asked, wanting to lead him into telling her all the things she never knew about where she lived.

"But our allies in Kenya believe there is more money in war and have been exposing us. This has put us in threat of war with the north and Asu Rah is leading the way, slowly making his way here." He took a deep breath.

"My father, the king, has made me general of the Tanzanian army and wants me to lead our men into battle against the armies of the north."

Kaleah's hands covered her mouth. "Oh no...."

"There's more." Zebadiah went to sit beside her and took her hands in his. "Please don't cry."

"I can't help it."

"Please, allow me to finish."

"What can be worse than you having to fight?"

He held his head low and kissed her hands.

"Our army alone is not enough to win against such a dominating power and my father and Ansuul Leer of Angola have put their differences aside to become a single force. This will bring all the armies of the east and south together for the greater good of all of Africa."

Kaleah searched Zebadiah's eyes and could see there was something harder for him to tell her about than having to lead his father's army.

"What is it? You're scaring me."

"In order for our nations to be truly united, the prince of Tanzania will marry the princess of Angola, and through the birth of a child the nations will be joined by both God and by blood."

Kaleah stood to her feet and tried to flee from her aching heart.

"I can't take this," she cried.

Zebadiah took her by her arm and turned her into him and he embraced her. She buried her head in his chest and cried heavily. She had never been asked to endure such pain. She pulled back and beat on his chest with her fists. He tried to continue to soothe her.

"Kaleah, I'm sorry."

"Be a man and tell your father, NO!"

"Kaleah, my hand will belong to another woman, my heart belongs to you, and my body will fight for Mother Africa."

"Fuck Africa! Let her defend herself. We can leave here and never return," she said passionately.

"You don't mean that. You're just upset and I know that."

Finally after a great deal of coaxing, Kaleah finally saw that the bigger picture had nothing to do with her man's heart. She didn't like it but as the Prince, and now the General of the Tanzanian army, he had a role to play and she would respect it as long as he stayed true to her.

"So when do you have to marry this bitch and go into her?"

Zebadiah had to crack a smile at her tenacity.

*****

"Soon. As we speak Asu is gathering his army, readying to make his move."

"So when did we come into play?" Shaka asked Daku, who was laid back in his recliner on the jet taking a break from the story of how their lives were created.

Daku pinched the bridge of his nose. "Rahmi..."

Rahmi was babysitting his glass of bourbon, intrigued with the way his brother retained the information he received only one month ago.

"Yes?"

"Do you mind picking up where I left off? I've become tired and wouldn't mind hearing the story again myself."

Shaka couldn't believe what he'd just heard Daku say.

"What? He knows more about where you came from more than you do?" But the way he said it sounded like he didn't want to hear his history told by no one else but his twin.

"It's not about the story brother and who tells it. It's about the journey. And we have a long way to go."

Stone added, "Shaka, have you ever held one of these?" he asked, tossing him a diamond the size of a strawberry.

Shaka caught it and was amazed at what he was holding.

"How many carats is this?" he asked excitedly, eyeballing the stone.

"That's only three hundred twenty-two. The record is something like 388.78 grams, found the year you were born."

"Damn, this bitch pretty as hell." Shaka looked at it again. "Is this pink?"

Stone nodded with a smile. "Yep. Pretty ain't she?"

"Hell yeah."

"Well, she's yours. I have twenty just like it."

Shaka looked up like, what the hell you doing with twenty of these?

"Straight up?"

"You will too. When Rahmi finishes telling you how you came to be in America, you'll appreciate what's yours even more than you do now."

Shaka was ready to listen to Rahmi with more enthusiasm and intensity than ever before. Daku looked at Stone and winked. Stone only nodded. Rahmi smiled, thinking that his brother and right hand man were clever, then got back to the story.

*****

"The war has been won, we have a beautiful daughter, and our families are sitting down at a huge feast enjoying the entertainment and finest of wines, why are you stuck in this room looking as if your world just ended?" the General asked.

Zakyra was perched on the breadth of an open window holding their daughter Danora. She was contemplating whether or not to talk to him about the discovery of him and his mistress, when in fact she did not know that it was she who had intruded into the web of happiness in his life. Instead she would hint at what was bothering her so that she didn't raise any red flags as to what she had planned for later on that evening.

Without looking at him she asked, "Do you think that me and Danora will ever be good enough for you to live life as a happy man?"

The General was confused. He walked over to the window and asked curiously, "Why would you ask that?"

"Because our marriage and our child were forced on you, we are not a choice but more so a contract. Our fathers, it's like we serve as only the handshake between them. That could have easily accomplished what all three of us stand for in this room."

The expression she chose to use was off the wall but yet was still truth at its best. She was hoping that the General would say something that would let her know that she was worth the love of him, but he did not. She wanted so badly, prayed that he would say something that would make her go back on the plans she had for his mistress, but he had no feelings for her and it was brutally obvious. Zakyra knew as a woman that men often got sidetracked and that if the object that was sidetracking them was, let's say, dead, then that may well draw them to the object that stands in front of them. So she sent the General back to his gathering without a quarrel and sent for Danora's caretaker while she put her plan into action.

Had the General told her he loved her and their daughter, she could have sent amnesties by her personal security to the rebels holding the General's mistress hostage and let her go to keep the General with a plaything as long as she never had to witness his adultery again. After all, she had her secrets with his brother, Prince Bontana, who was the one who told her about his affair with the mistress whom she now knew to be Kaleah. To this day only two people know how Zakyra found out. On her way out the city she thought it was better to build up her courage by getting drunk off wine because in her sober state she had none. So as her security drove, she drank and made herself hate Kaleah.

Kaleah hung by her wrists roped together between two poles and one welded across the top, naked and gagged. Her swollen titties and pregnant belly glistened with sweat. Even her

legs looked oiled, tragically beautiful from a twisted mind point
of view.

When Zakyra made it in to where she was being held
captive, she finally knew what her kidnapping was about.

Zakyra was smoking a cigarette and pacing around her.
Kaleah was nervous as ever and Zakyra was making it worse by
not saying a word. Seeing Kaleah's bulging belly was pissing her
off and she wanted the baby out. She would then kill her and
that would be the end of it. But she was still too weak of a
person to murder another human, so she pumped herself up by
slapping Kaleah hard across her face repeatedly while saying
incoherent things in an off-the-wall language no one in the
room knew. Finally, in her bloodthirsty rage, she told the rebels
to hold Kaleah's legs apart at the ankles. She snatched Kaleah's
head back by her hair.

Kaleah was sweating heavily and her breathing was deep
and erratic. Her eyes grew wide looking at the crazed Zakyra
snap.

"So you wanna have his baby, huh? Is that it?" she growled.

Zakyra took a few steps back and kicked Kaleah so hard in
the pussy even God flinched.

Kaleah had never felt such pain. Being murdered ten times
couldn't compare and before the pain could fully register,
another kick to the pussy came, followed by another and
another. It was hard for the rebels to hold on to her legs with

blood spattering across their faces. They were actually entertained by the muffled screams of Kaleah until she took a bloody shit and they let go of her legs.

Zakyra was pissed. "What are you doing? Hold her!" she commanded.

"She took a shit. I'll kill but I'm not touching shit," the man holding Kaleah's left leg said pointing.

"Uuhhh." Zakyra let out a roar of frustration and kicked Kaleah again in the pussy. The kick was vicious and must have dilated Kaleah a full eight centimeters because her baby's head popped out and it was ready to drop.

Zakyra was wiping sweat from her forehead when she looked down and noticed it. When she did, she became mad all over again. She walked over to Kaleah and snatched the baby outta her by its head. You could hear her flesh tearing like a zipper as it happened.

"You think you can just have my husband's baby?" she yelled and snatched the umbilical cord from Kaleah's pussy like a telephone wire out the wall. There was a vicious pop sound.

But in the end, Zakyra still couldn't bring herself to murder so she gave the babe, who is Daku today, to the rebels to dispose of and banished Kaleah to only God knows where. But Bontana found her and brought her to the village. All of us on the border of Kenya sought refuge when we refused to fight for the rebels Zakyra had put together. To this day, no one fully knows her plan, but a portion of it was to kill Daku.

"Why?" Shaka asked.

"Because..." Rahmi started.

"Because with me gone, Danora would be the only blood of the General to take heir of his legacy, which are the diamond mines, our army, our land, and the mineral rights of all our lands."

"But she is the first born from what I understand," Shaka said with a haze of confusion.

"True, but she is not a son."

Shaka nodded in understanding.

"We are princes, you and I."

"So where was I in all of this?"

"When Kaleah was released, she held you inside herself until she was clear of any danger then had you in a pond near her sister's house. There they agreed to keep you a secret and the only way to do that was to get you the farthest away from Africa. So Kaleah took every ounce of money she had and gave it to her sister Rebeccah to take you to America. She, along with her husband, Farheed, changed their names to Ciara and Marcus and yours to Bryce. They took you away from Africa so that one day you could come back and rule because they thought Daku was dead. They wanted you to return one day and exact revenge for this side of your family, for what Zakyra had done."

"I get it," Shaka said knowingly.

"So one of the rebels who threw my brother away later confessed that when he went back to see if Daku was dead he didn't know because Daku's body was gone. Apparently, nine or so years had gone by before he said anything. Zakyra got wind of it and sent them to finish the job, to kill every male that age in Tanzania while at the same time murking anybody that refused to join the rebels. The hunt led her to information about Kaleah having a sister who fled to the United States with a baby, and the search ended with them African ma'fucka's finding me, not knowing that I'm not the one the rebels threw away because Kaleah had twins. The General knew because he was looking at himself when he saw Daku at the camp and had also gotten wind of the same story Zakyra did about me being in America. So that made him know that there were two of us."

All three heads nodded in unison. Stone smiled. "Daku, he is very smart, this one."

"Indeed," Daku replied.

"But what happened to Zakyra?" Shaka asked.

No one said anything. Daku looked out the window. Rahmi downed his third drink and Stone sat back in his chair.

When all three men made it back to the mansion in Tanzania, Africa, there were six people in the living room to greet them. Ciara, Marcus, Abdu, Bontana, Kaleah, and the General.

Daku's jaw almost hit the floor.

"My sons," the General said excitedly with open arms as he stood to go hug them.

"I thought you said this nigga was dead," Shaka said.

BLOOD STONE 2: THE THRILL
COMING SOON

.

Also Available From Rhys World Publishing

Love Truth And Consequence By Author Taisha Demay

The Journeys We Take In Life By Author Rosa Arnold

Reign Of Terror By Author Arthur Battle

Squad Up By Author Arthur Battle

Pushed To The Limit By Author Arthur Battle

Kross Out By Author Rhys Flint

Juug Men By Author Rhys Flint

Gun Buy By Author Rhys Flint

Yung Gunz By Author Wolfgang Gill

Laces By Author Black Rose

Coming Soon

Taste Of Intrigue By Author Taisha Demay

Clouded Judgment 2 By Author Byron Carey

Just A Vacancy By Lissha Sadler (Short)

Love Unplugged: The B Side Of Love Series By Author DE Adams

www.ingramcontent.com/pod-product-compliance
Lightning Source LLC
Chambersburg PA
CBHW070815180626
46818CB00001B/280